After three years of waiting, Drew Britton wanted to set the record straight.

"I bought the old Chappie cabin, Marnette," he said slowly and deliberately, as if to give her time for it to finally sink in—all he had said earlier about the fireplace and the well and adding some rooms. "I bought it for us."

She opened her mouth as if to protest, but he cut her short.

"Don't tell me any more lies, Marnie. I know you love me."

"No." It was barely above a whisper.

Even as she said it, Marnette knew it was another lie. But the biggest lie was the one she had so long been telling herself. No matter what Drew Britton had done when he himself had been only sixteen, he had carved his name on her heart the very day they had met.

"We've wasted too much time already, Marnie," he told her. "I don't want to waste any more."

And he didn't.

MARY LA PIETRA is the author of eight children's books and three award-winning children's plays. *His Name on Her Heart* is her second inspirational romance, but her debut novel with **Heartsong Presents**.

Don't miss out on any of our super romances. Write to us at the following address for information on our newest releases and club information.

Heartsong Presents Readers' Service
P.O. Box 719
Uhrichsville, OH 44683

His Name on
Her Heart

Mary La Pietra

Heartsong Presents

A note from the Author:

I love to hear from my readers! You may write to me at the following address:

> **Mary La Pietra**
> **Author Relations**
> **P.O. Box 719**
> **Uhrichsville, OH 44683**

ISBN 1-55748-688-3

HIS NAME ON HER HEART

PRINTED IN THE U.S.A.

one

Fanning herself with her open spelling book, Marnette Coulter was tempted to open another button in the yoke of her prim gray schoolteacher's frock. But she dared not offer any scandal to the twelve sweltering students waiting for their temporary "schoolmarm" to give them the next word to scratch out on their slates. Two of them gave her wry smiles when, without even looking at the book, she switched the word from "incurable" to "unbearable."

Her grandmother had been right. Even before the spring thaw, Ina Coulter had predicted they were in for a "two washdays summer"—that it would be so hot, the usual Monday wash day would not be enough to keep her hard-working family in fresh linens.

But it was not only the heat that Marnette found so unbearable this early June morning; it was all that racket just beyond the schoolyard: hammer striking nail, nail biting into wood. And that brain-jolting clatter as another barrowful of bricks was dumped onto the hard ground.

Marnette was sure the schoolmaster, so long on temporary leave, would be pleased with the men's progress: that with the building of a town hall in this Year of Our Lord, 1848, Chappie Creek was finally becoming "civilized." But wouldn't even Stuart Whittington, a pillar of self-control, have been rattled by all that racket?

She got up from the desk and walked with her book to the nearest window, sorely tempted to close it. But she dared not shut any of the six schoolhouse windows, not in such suffocating heat. She looked out the window and then quickly drew

5

back. There had been many curious customs for her to accept when she had come to the small prairie town three years ago. Perhaps the most perplexing was its being a scandal for a young unmarried woman to gaze upon such blatant masculine bareness.

But it was not the fear of any sin that kept Marnette Coulter from another glance out the window. It was the knowledge that one of those bare-chested workers, sawing lumber but a few yards from the window, had seen her. And she had gone to great pains never to give Drew Britton the idea that she might be the least bit interested in him—with or without a shirt.

Her face was even more flushed when she went back to her desk. "I'll check those slates later," she told her students. And she heard a dozen sighs of relief as she closed her spelling book.

Hoping it might be easier on their poor overheated brains, Marnette had decided to read to them, and she reached for one of the three gold-embossed books propped up between two discarded bricks she had picked up from the schoolyard earlier that week. She never opened one of those books that she didn't wonder about the town's long-absent schoolmaster.

It was all of six months since Stuart Whittington had taken the stagecoach east to do whatever he had to do as executor of his late uncle's estate. The school board had readily agreed that Marnette Coulter—the only other person in town, besides the doctor, to have had a "higher education"—should take over at the schoolhouse in his absence. Happy to be relieved of some of the tedious chores at her own uncle's cabin, Marnette had just as readily agreed.

"Two months at most," Mister Whittington had assured her, and Marnette could only wonder if he had included travel time in that estimate. For those two months had stretched into six, and there had not been a single word from the bewhiskered schoolmaster since he had climbed onto the stage. Unless

Marnette was to consider the three finely-tooled leather books as being a "word."

Not too long after she had pinned up her long black hair and taken her temporary post as schoolmarm, *The Works of Charles and Mary Lamb* had been delivered at the schoolhouse by Trader Farnsworth's grandson. The brown paper-wrapped parcel had been addressed to "The Chappie Creek Schoolmarm," and all the breathless delivery boy could add was that it had "come from Boston."

The second book—a small volume of verse by John Keats— had arrived a month later, addressed in the same manner and again brought to the schoolhouse by the trader's grandson. Marnette had found the third book, *The Compleat Works of William Shakespeare,* on her uncle's doorstep one Saturday morning.

Though she had not the slightest doubt that each of the books was from Stuart Whittington, she was surprised by his choice of literature. She had never dreamed the bachelor schoolmaster, such a stern dispenser of dictum and discipline, might be so romantic.

Having herself resolved never to become involved with any man, only once did Marnette ponder her own paradoxical delight in daily reading small snatches of *Romeo and Juliet* to her students. And she told herself it was only the late bard's masterful use of rhythm and rhyme that so captivated her.

Besides, it was good to have something other than the McGuffey readers and the Bible as teaching tools. By now the children probably knew all those moralistic McGuffey stories by heart, and she was sure they had ample exposure to the Good Book both at home and at church every Sunday.

Now it was Marnette herself who loudly sighed. Today, in such stifling heat, even re-reading Shakespeare's impassioned balcony scene suddenly lost its charm. And, without even opening it, she slid the master's leather-bound "works" back between the other two expensive books from Stuart Whittington.

She looked with pity at the students he had left in her charge, the two girls as bedraggled as the ten boys. They would squirm and sweat for another whole week before the official end of the school term. And how much would even the brightest of them learn with all that wood-sawing, brick-dumping racket outside?

"Students," she told them, "you've all behaved so well in this dreadful noise and heat, I think you should be rewarded. We won't have any more lessons today. In fact—" she suddenly decided at the clatter of yet another dumped load of bricks, "school is now closed for the summer. You may all go home—and stay home—right now."

With one joyful whoop, slates were suddenly slapped aside, and there was a mad scramble for the schoolhouse door—the girls as eager as the boys. Marnette smiled, as outside their happy shouts mingled with the whack of nail-driving hammers.

In her mind, she also heard the relieved sighs of some of their parents. Especially the two chore-weary mothers who had reluctantly surrendered their oldest girls to "waste their time" at the schoolhouse, learning to read and write.

Mister Whittington, too, held onto the ancient notion that a girl's brain was too weak for learning. Even so, she doubted he would have been pleased with her dismissing any of his twelve students a week early.

So be it, she sighed. It was over and done with and there was no way that she could undo it. Besides, he could always open the schoolhouse a week earlier in September—for surely the schoolmaster would be back in town by then.

As for Marnette herself, the early dismissal was a blessing. Now she would have more time to work on those fancy gowns she had agreed to make for some of the ladies to wear at the Founders' Day ball in August, sewing at a more leisurely pace—

those tiny, almost invisible stitches that were the hallmark of her other, more permanent occupation: that of Chappie Creek's most sought-after seamstress.

The very dress she herself was now wearing—plain gray calico with white lace trim at the collar and wrists—had been cut and sewn with that same meticulous care. But in this case, she had been careful, too, that the bodice did not fit as well as it should. *What man*, she had reasoned, *would bother giving a second glance to a frumpy, sack-frocked schoolmarm?*

She had gotten the disconcerting answer to that the first time she had passed Doc Britton's bare-chested son, sawing lumber in the schoolyard. Which was why she had begun taking the long way to and from school, going through the woods and coming into and out of the schoolhouse by its back door.

Marnette now left her platformed desk to collect the dozen happily surrendered slates from the students' benches. She smiled at their earnest efforts—only the girls had gotten it right—in trying to spell "unbearable."

After wiping each of the slates clean with a piece of chamois, she stacked them on the middle shelf of the large oak cabinet at the rear of the room. There, along with the tin of stubby chalk, the dozen McGuffey readers, and the empty water pail and dipper, they would be stored until September.

Whether it was the first day of school or the last, Marnette always had to pack away the schoolroom paraphernalia because the one-room white frame building also served the townsfolk as their church on Sunday. And, until the new town hall was finished, both the school board and the Chappie Creek Town Council meetings would also still be held at the schoolhouse. Indeed, this very night the seven town councilmen were to hold a special "closed" meeting to appoint both a town clerk and a town constable—yet another step in the town's becoming "civilized."

Before closing the big cabinet, Marnette took out the

wood-handled carpetbag that she carried to and from the school-house each day. The same bag that had accompanied her, three years ago, on the incoming stagecoach.

She set the bag on the schoolmaster's desk to begin filling it with her own personal items, first and foremost the three precious books he had sent her from Boston. She thought of discarding the two chipped brick bookends, but then also slipped them into the bag. Set near the fire this winter, they would come in handy as bed warmers.

Winter, she sighed. *How wonderful to feel one of those icy blasts just now.*

Next, she opened the desk's only drawer to take out her yet unopened lunch pail and her precious comb, hairbrush, and mirror. On impulse, she glanced into the pearl-handled mirror, only to loudly sigh again.

No matter how tightly she wound her long black hair into that matronly bun, there were always a few renegade ringlets over her brow and before each ear. And it would take nothing short of a widow's veil to hide those wistful, doe-brown eyes and those long, sultry lashes—that dusky complexion and that seemingly kiss-puckered mouth. Despite all her efforts at looking like a dowdy old maid, she looked no more, nor any less, than her almost twenty years—ripe and ready for marriage.

"You're not fooling anyone with that spinster's bun, Marnette," her cousin Emilie had told her that morning as she was fixing her hair before the mirror in their shared bedroom. "Or that sacky dress, either."

Marnette's only response had been shoving another hairpin into the bun. She already knew Emilie didn't believe her excuse for the ill-fitting dress and the old-maidish bun: so everyone in town, and more especially her twelve captive students, would take their petite "schoolmarm" seriously.

"Prettiest girl in town," said Emilie, "and you act as if it's a curse."

Marnette still didn't answer. But she was thinking: *Curse? Yes, that was a good word for it.* To have both a face and a figure that turned all the men's heads—even in church—wasn't that a curse for any young woman who had vowed never to marry?

"I don't know what happened back East to make you so sour on men," Emilie had also told her that morning, "but this I do know. There isn't a woman on the prairie who doesn't sooner or later need a man. In fact, you wouldn't even be here if it weren't for a certain wonderful man."

Marnette could not deny that. Indeed, if Doc Britton had not accidentally found her in Boston, she might still be homelessly wandering the city's streets.

two

Her grandmother still called it one of "God's timely miracles," that Doc Britton had been in Boston for a seminar—and more especially had come to the boarding school—the very day Marnette was being dismissed.

Though Marnette agreed that the timing had been right, she was sure it had merely been a coincidence and had happened only because God had been looking the other way. She was also sure her other grandmother would have agreed.

Not only had Marnette been totally ignorant of having any other relatives in the world, her prairie kinfolk also hadn't known she had ever been born. If they had—especially Grandma Ina Coulter—perhaps Marnette's childhood wouldn't have been so wretched. And she wouldn't have spent those last six years as a prisoner in that stuffy boarding school.

Even Doc Britton, the very one who had found her, did not know her dreadful history and the truth about her father's death. Or the even uglier truth about her mother's.

She would never forget the day she had come down from the school dormitory and found the morning newspaper beside her breakfast plate. The entire front page was all about the fire two nights before. Inside, there was a half-page editorial, righteously claiming it had been the wrath of God.

Barely a week later, on a rainy Friday night, the headmistress told Marnette to pack her bag. Indeed, Marnette was surprised it had taken the school's upright board of directors that long to issue the order for her dismissal. Unless they had not been absolutely certain about her mother—not until the money for Marnette's monthly tuition had not been slipped under the back door.

Whatever, it seemed they could not get rid of her fast enough. Especially the headmistress, who herself helped Marnette empty her wardrobe and pack her bag.

And though with her students, Miss Veasley had always been a stickler for decorum and propriety, Marnette had not missed the woman's unmuffled muttering of "good riddance to bad rubbish" behind her as she lugged the heavy carpetbag down the bannistered stairs. Which really did not surprise her. If Marnette had learned anything at the Beacon Hill Academy for Young Women, it was that money covered a multitude of sins. And it had not mattered that her tuition money might be tainted, so long as it kept coming the first of every month.

She had barely reached the bottom of the stairs when Katie Sullivan, the school's plump, red-faced Irish cook, rushed out of the kitchen to make a last-minute plea that Marnette be allowed to stay on at the school, earning her keep by working in the kitchen.

"She has nowhere else to go," she reminded the headmistress. "And the Lord knows, I could use some help in the kitchen."

Alma Veasley gave the cook a cold stare, one of the rare times her mouth was silent. Indeed, sometimes even the haughtiest of doctors' daughters could be heard snickering behind the door at the constant "click" of the headmistress' store-bought teeth. Marnette doubted they would laugh, though, if they knew she always opened and then re-sealed the girls' incoming mail.

"The matter is totally out of my hands," the headmistress told Katie Sullivan. Marnette understood what the problem was. When she was a paid-up student—regardless of how the money had been earned—no one had denied her a place among the other girls at the academy's long dining room table. But as a penniless helper in the school's kitchen, the daughter of

Cynthia Coulter would surely contaminate the food.

"Ah, yes," Katie nodded in Gaelic sarcasm, "it was decided by all those church-going saints on the board. And may the Lord slam the gates of heaven in all of your Pharisee faces, for sendin' the poor girl out in this rain!"

It was not the first of such irreverent outbursts from the feisty little immigrant, overlooked because there was not another cook in Boston who could perform the magic she did on the stingy food budget the school board allotted her.

But apparently this latest of Irish curses gave the headmistress second thoughts. "You may wait in the foyer," she told Marnette before turning toward her office. "Until the rain stops."

Only months later, when she allowed herself to think back on it, did Marnette realize that the two women—Katie Sullivan with her last-ditch plea and Alma Veasley, magnanimously allowing her to sit out the rain—had played such crucial roles in what her prairie grandmother called a miracle.

For it was while Marnette was in the academy foyer, waiting out the rain, that the two doctors had walked in the front door. One of them had come to take his daughter home for the weekend, and the other, in Boston for a seminar on modern-day medicine, was to have dinner with them that evening.

The latter had almost passed her, seated on the bench beside her carpetbag, when he suddenly turned.

"Emilie?" he asked in astonishment. For, to this very day, some people in Chappie Creek had trouble telling one cousin from the other, especially in passing.

But Marnette hadn't known she had a cousin—three, in fact—as well as an uncle and a grandmother living out on the prairie. As far as she knew, the only family she had were now all dead.

And she was sure the tall and handsome bearded doctor realized he had mistaken her for someone else. Especially after he bent to get a closer look at her face. "No, it isn't Emilie—is it?"

She confirmed that with a shake of her head. "It's Marnette."

"But it must be Coulter," he insisted.

Marnette could never recall exactly what happened after that: who said what and at what point she began believing the doctor. Indeed, Claymore Britton himself twice marveled aloud at such a "lucky twist of fate"—that he should have so accidentally stumbled upon Ina Coulter's orphaned granddaughter. Especially when none of the Coulters knew she had been born.

But Marnette's somewhat reluctant confession, on the boarding school bench, to being the daughter of Thomas Coulter had clinched it. For, back in Chappie Creek, Ina Coulter had never stopped hoping for some word of her Boston-born, seafaring son, Thomas, missing for over twenty years.

Marnette still wondered what would have become of her— where she would have gone—if Doc Britton had not walked in the door of the Beacon Hill Academy that rainy night. For it had rained the entire night that she spent with him at the other doctor's house. And it was still raining the next day when she and Doc Britton climbed into the stagecoach that would take them to Albany, New York, where they would begin their weeks-long journey that would bring Marnette Coulter home to her new-found family in Chappie Creek.

"If she swoons," the doctor said with a twinkle in his green eyes, "at least she'll have a doctor on hand to revive her." He meant, of course, Marnette's yet unsuspecting grandmother. "Though I wish I could give her better news about your father," he added with a comforting squeeze of Marnette's gloved hand.

The news that Ina Coulter would receive was that Marnette's father had died a hero's death at sea, seven years ago. And that her mother had succumbed, only a week ago, to tuberculosis. The two quickly manufactured lies Marnette would tell again and again in Chappie Creek.

It was all like some fanciful bedtime story. And though it would be some time before Marnette believed it was actually happening, she had already vowed not to spoil such a nice story with the ugly truth.

Having never once set foot outside Boston, Marnette had no idea of the vast wilderness that lay west of that crowded seaport city or of how long she and the doctor would travel before reaching Chappie Creek.

While the overland stagecoach trip to Albany was slow enough, the second phase of their long westward journey was even slower: by packet boat—pulled by horses from the bank—down some curious inland waterway her companion told her was the Erie Canal.

Then, at a place called Buffalo, the packet hoisted its sails, and the sailor's daughter suffered her first bout of seasickness as the boat entered the waters of Lake Erie to finally deposit her and the doctor on land for the longest and most arduous leg of their journey—again by stagecoach—to Chappie Creek.

It was then, as she stared out the coach window, that Marnette was struck by the vastness and the wildness of the land, the countless miles of open prairie, only now and then broken by a distant grove of trees, a solitary weather-beaten farmhouse, and an occasional rotting wooden trail marker to assure her that someone else, indeed, had dared to venture this far from civilization.

But neither those farmhouses nor those trail markers were of any comfort the day the stagecoach rumbled past a small band of buckskinned braves on horseback at the side of the road. Though the Indians only stone-facedly stared at the white man's ridiculous rolling box, Marnette felt every hair on her head suddenly come alive.

Sitting beside her in the stagecoach, Doc Britton apparently sensed her fear. And again she felt his comforting hand on hers, tightly clenched in her lap.

"Only a band of hunters," he assured her, "out for skins to swap at the nearest trading post."

Though the Indians' "swapping" anything with the white man sounded harmless enough, Marnette was relieved when she again looked out the window and the band of buckskinned watchers was gone.

੨ઠ

The stagecoach picked up and dropped off a number of other travelers along the way, but by the time it made its last stop before Chappie Creek at Trapper's Bend—a combined trading post, livery stable, and two-story roadhouse at a bend in the dusty road—Marnette and the handsome country doctor were its only passengers.

And apparently they were somewhat late, for their hosts, Abner and Molly Trippet, were waiting for them out on the porch of the frame roadhouse.

Though the couple's greeting was warm enough, they were barely in the door when Marnette sensed Molly Trippet's coldness toward the doctor before hustling her upstairs for a hot bath, Marnette's first full bath since leaving Boston.

"Proves what they say," the woman muttered, handing Marnette a towel. "That you can't always tell the corn by its husk."

Marnette was sure she was talking about Doc Britton. "Then you know him?"

The woman begrudgingly nodded. "Stopped here on his way east. Said he was bound for some big doctors' meeting in Boston. Would never in my life have dreamed what he really was up to."

She helped Marnette towel herself dry. A bit more roughly than was necessary, Marnette thought, not knowing the roughness was meant for the doctor.

"The question is," said Molly, "how much do you know about

him?"

"Not much," Marnette admitted. But she did know one thing: Doctor Claymore Britton was the only man in her life she had ever allowed herself to trust. "I only met him the day before we left."

"And you packed up and went—just like that?"

"I was already packed."

Molly shook her head. "Unbelievable."

"Yes," Marnette nodded, "it is a rather strange story."

"They always are." Molly again shook her head. "And there ought to be a law against it," she muttered before going downstairs to dish up the dinner she had so long been keeping warm.

The meal was on the table when Marnette finally came down in her very last fresh dress. After she sat down, across the table from Doc Britton, she wondered if Molly Trippet hadn't given her the wrong plate. Heaped with boiled potatoes, salt pork, and collard greens, it was more than double the portion on the doctor's plate. But she decided it really didn't matter. For even though Molly had given her husband and the coach driver equally hefty helpings, there still was plenty in the big serving bowls.

Marnette had barely picked up her fork when her hostess again began muttering to herself. "Scrub her knuckles to the bone keeping his cabin clean, give him a nice fat baby, and then crawl into her grave with childbed fever. No better off than one of those poor Indian squaws."

Though Molly's husband and the driver merely kept on eating, the doctor looked up from his skimpy plateful to give his hostess a clinical look from across the table, as if wondering whether she might not have a case of cabin fever, something Marnette knew could happen, even in Boston, when a person was cooped up indoors too long. More so, in such a lonely prairie outpost as Trapper's Bend.

Molly's next mutterings were something about "such a sweet

young thing" going to live in "such an awful place" like Chappie Creek.

Apparently having decided to take care of his own case—that of a still-empty stomach—the doctor reached for the potato bowl while asking Molly what was so awful about Chappie Creek.

"As if you didn't know," she snorted, openly moving the potato bowl out of his reach.

"Know what?" Marnette dared to ask. After all, she would—if she were accepted by her prairie family—be spending the rest of her life in Chappie Creek.

It was Molly's husband, Abner, who answered her around a mouthful of collard greens. "Hoard of redskins killed off more than half of 'em a while back."

"A whole lot more than a while back," said Doc Britton, eyeing the out-of-reach potato bowl. "Over twenty years ago."

Molly now also moved the platter of pork some distance away. "It's bad enough taking a child as your bride—but to a desolate outpost like Chappie Creek?"

At the word "bride," Marnette almost choked on her own mouthful of greens. She suddenly understood the woman's questions upstairs and all her muttering at the dinner table, as well as her obvious attempts to starve Marnette's handsome, middle-aged escort.

Though she had led an almost cloistered life the past six years at the Boston boarding school, Marnette had heard of men going west to settle a homestead and then advertising back east for a wife. Molly apparently thought Marnette was such a "mail-order" bride.

While the mistake almost floored Marnette, it obviously tickled the doctor. "Tied to an old duffer like me?" he chuckled, winking at Marnette across the table. "I'd have all the young bucks back in town wanting to lynch me."

He leaned forward, as if determined to get his hands on some more food. But their hostess, apparently having found him innocent, was already handing him the potato bowl.

"Besides," the doctor added soberly, "I've already put two wives in an early grave—I wouldn't chance making it three."

៙

Not long after their meal, the weary but well-fed travelers all went to bed: the doctor and the driver in one room, and Marnette alone in another.

But though the featherbed and goose down pillow were the softest of any on their several stage stops, Marnette had trouble falling asleep.

She was not sure what bothered her most: that the doctor had not told her anything about a massacre in Chappie Creek, or that Molly Trippet had mistaken them for husband and wife.

three

Chappie Creek finally emerged on the horizon, at a distance looking much like the dozen or so other towns Marnette and the doctor had passed through once they had reached the open flatlands: hardly more than a string of log cabins, a general store, and a hitching post.

But as they drew nearer, Marnette could see there was more to this prairie town than the last one they had passed through: several white frame buildings, one of them with a steeple which did anything but quell her growing apprehension. There had been churches in Boston, too, and thinking of one of them always made her feel sick.

Doc Britton apparently read the look on her face as disappointment at the town where she was likely to spend the rest of her life.

"It's no Boston," he told her, "but it's no desolate outpost, either."

Marnette was sorry she had made him feel the need to defend the town where he was the only doctor, especially since he was the only reason she was not wandering homeless on the streets of Boston.

But as the stagecoach rattled into town, the doctor was anything but defensive in pointing out some of the town's thriving businesses: the grist mill and the saw mill, the blacksmith's and barber's shops.

Though it all seemed pitifully backwoods compared to Boston, Marnette tried to look as if she were truly impressed.

"And maybe someday a telegraph office, too," the doctor added.

21

Marnette knew that would be a boon for any prairie town. Like most of the other towns they had passed through, Chappie Creek's only communication with any points east was by the mail carried in canvas bags atop the monthly stagecoach. Certainly no hardship for Marnette Coulter, since there was no one back East likely to write her a letter.

While the stagecoach had had the run of the open road, once they entered the town's square that Saturday morning, the driver had to carefully steer the coach between other horses and wagons as well as buckskinned men and bonneted women on foot, bustling about in all directions.

Their long journey finally ended at a broad, porch-fronted log building with an equally broad chiseled wood sign that proclaimed it the Chappie Creek General Store & Trading Post.

Even before the stage had completely rolled to a stop, two young women who had been waiting on the porch ran up to the coach crying, "Pa!" at which Doc Britton bolted out to catch them both in a bone-crushing hug.

Watching, Marnette felt a sudden ache in her heart—the same ache she had always felt back at the boarding school when the other girls so joyously flew down the stairs to greet their fathers, come to take them home for the holidays. This was the way it was with a true family.

Only when the family broke their embrace did Marnette see the striking difference in the doctor's two girls: one with hair the color of corn silk and the other with two long, raven-black braids. Though he had confessed to putting two wives in an early grave, he had not hinted that one of them had been an Indian or that either of those women had borne him any children.

Silently and somewhat jealously watching the little family reunion, Marnette was not aware of a third member in the welcoming party. Not until the tall, flaxen-haired young man also stepped down from the porch, holding out his right hand.

"Welcome home, Pa."

Doc Britton heartily shook his son's hand. "Good to be back, Drew."

The doctor then glanced about the town square, as if to make sure nothing had changed while he had been away. "No major calamities while I was gone?"

"Only Trader Farnsworth," said his son with a backward nod toward the trading post. "Totally ran out of gossip for a whole day."

All four of them laughed at that, and again Marnette felt a jealous pang. She had never shared a little joke with anyone, not even the other schoolgirls' snickers at the click of the head-mistress' false teeth.

"And we had a big windstorm last week that took even Grandma Coulter by surprise," said the fairer of the doctor's daughters.

"And she's in for another surprise," said Doc Britton, turning back toward the stagecoach.

It was only then that the welcomers became aware of another passenger, still seated in the coach. Marnette had begun to think the doctor himself had forgotten about her.

"Drew, go help the little lady down."

"Yes, sir." His son obediently came to the stagecoach and opened the door. And when he held out his hand, Marnette found herself looking into the same green-eyed, good-humored face as that of the man she had so dangerously come close to loving. Only younger. And beardless. And even handsomer.

While she was taken aback at Drew Britton's resemblance to his father, he was even more stunned by her likeness to someone else in town. "Emilie?" he said incredulously.

"No, not Emilie," said Doc Britton as Marnette, taking Drew's offered hand, shyly stepped down from the coach. "Her cousin, Marnette, from Boston," the doctor explained without the tiniest trace of doubt.

"I didn't know Emilie *had* a cousin," said his yellow-haired daughter.

"Emilie doesn't know it yet, either," he said wryly. He then glanced at his tall, look-alike son who was silently staring down at the mysterious Coulter cousin whose hand had, only moments ago, been in his. "You bring the buckboard, Drew?"

"Yes, sir."

"Fine. Get my satchel down—and this little lady's bag, too. I want to get her out to the Coulters in time for lunch."

❧

His family had to wait for the story—how he had found Marnette at the Boston boarding school—until they were all in the buckboard, heading out to the Coulter farm: the doctor gripping the reins, his hatless, blue-shirted son beside him on the driver's seat, and their long-skirted and bonneted cargo behind, on a bench-like wooden plank that ran along one side of the wagon bed.

Marnette, between the two Britton sisters, silently sat through the doctor's lost-and-found story, uneasy at being its main character and again resolving that no one in Chappie Creek—not even the doctor himself—would ever know the whole story.

She also felt out of place in her velvet-trimmed paisley traveling suit, wrinkled and dusty though it might be—a sore contrast to the plain calico frocks of the two prairie town sisters whose names she had yet to learn.

"She certainly does look a lot like Emilie," the fair one agreed at the end of her father's on-the-road tale of the almost homeless granddaughter.

"Only smaller," said her brother with a backward glance. "And prettier."

An innocent enough remark, but it set off a little warning bell in Marnette's brain. She would have to be on guard against this good-looking son of Doc Britton.

Somewhere along the bumpy buckboard ride out of town, one of the doctor's daughters suddenly realized they had not been properly introduced.

"I'm Abbie," she told Marnette. "Short for Abigail. Andrew and I are twins," she added with a nod toward her brother.

Marnette dared not so much as glance in his direction. Besides she had already thought they might be twins—even though features so striking in a young man were so plain in a girl.

"I am Wilting Sunflower," the darker girl smiled. While her half-Indian face was anything but plain, Marnette thought there was, indeed, something a bit wilted in her smile. She had also noticed the girl walked with a slight limp.

"Marnette," the white girl mused aloud. "I don't believe I've ever heard that name before."

"It's really Marie Antoinette," Marnette explained. "But all of my friends back East called me Marnette."

They were the very first words out of her mouth since stepping down from the stagecoach, and already she had told a lie. But who would believe that Marnette Coulter had had only one true friend in her entire life: Katie Sullivan, her feisty but unsuccessful advocate back at the boarding school. The only person Marnette was sure she would miss from her life back in Boston. Even so, the longer they traveled over the wheel-rutted road to her uncle's farm, the more anxious Marnette grew about what lay ahead. How would her yet unsuspecting Chappie Creek family take her sudden appearance?

"I can't wait to see their faces," said Doc Britton, as if able to read her mind.

"Especially her grandmother," said Abbie.

The doctor nodded. "It'll be the first time anyone ever sneaked up on that shrewd little squaw."

He glanced back just in time to catch Marnette's look of surprise at the word *squaw.*

"Half Indian, too," he told her.

Marnette shouldn't have been so surprised. Hadn't she thought her father's skin was darker than most? And hadn't she often wondered about her own?

"Though there are some folks in town who swear the other half of Ina Coulter is witch," the doctor chuckled. "She can tell you what you're thinking before you're even thinking it."

At this, Marnette felt her heart sink. Would this mind-reading grandmother swallow her story, as Doc Britton had, that her father had been lost at sea and her mother had finally died of consumption? But why shouldn't she?

And even if someone else in town didn't believe it—and wrote to the boarding school to verify her story—Marnette was sure that Alma Veasley, ever concerned with preserving the reputation of such an upright institution, would not call Marnette Coulter a liar.

"But you'll not find a truer, gospel-living Christian this side of the Mississippi," the doctor added in defense of Marnette's yet-to-be-met prairie grandmother.

That statement did nothing to ease Marnette's anxiety. She had another grandmother—now under the sod in a Boston church cemetery—who had also been known as a good, Bible-quoting Christian. And her last words to Marnette and her mother, on the steps of that church, made the worst of Katie Sullivan's Irish curses sound like a blessing.

Marnette wished now that she hadn't just packed up and gone with the country doctor. That she might have at least asked him questions about Thaddeus Coulter, her father's brother and the farmer under whose cabin roof she would be living. If two cousins could be so much alike, wouldn't the same be even more true of their fathers? She shuddered at the thought.

The three girls suddenly lurched sideways as the buckboard came to a stop.

"There she is, Marnette," said Doc Britton. "Your new home."

While she had observed a number of log cabins on their way into town and had had serious doubts about living in any one of them, Marnette was relieved at the size of the Coulter cabin, set about twenty yards back from the road.

"Biggest in town," said the doctor. "Three whole rooms."

Marnette knew that even a two-room log cabin was something to boast about. Still, she wondered if the farmer's family would have room—in either their home or their hearts—for this orphaned stranger.

"I'd better go in first," the doctor said, "and set them up for the big surprise."

"We'll go in, too," said Abbie, meaning herself and her half sister. "It's been almost a week since we've seen Emilie."

The doctor nodded his approval before climbing down and tying the reins to the roadside hitching post. "Drew, you give us about ten minutes and then help our little lady down and bring her in."

"Yes, sir," his son quickly replied. A bit too quickly for Marnette.

She watched as the two sisters hitched up their skirts and climbed down, unassisted, from the wagon. And just as silently watched as they walked, with their father, up the long footpath to her uncle's cabin.

Ten minutes. More like ten years, sitting alone on the wagon bench with Drew Britton's back to her. She had no way of knowing, then, what a rare thing it was for the doctor's son to be at a loss for words and that it was only to cover that loss that he took out his jackknife and began chipping away at a small piece of wood—all the while softly whistling.

She wondered what was going on inside the cabin. Had her grandmother fainted at the news? Or worse, was she telling Doc Britton to take his homeless baggage somewhere else?

"It's time," Drew suddenly announced, though Marnette hadn't seen him look at any watch. He closed his jackknife and shoved it and his carving back into his pocket. He then jumped down from the seat and stood at the side of the wagon, ready to help her down.

Marnette sat as if glued to the long wooden bench. For, though it had taken only his hand to help her out of the stagecoach, she knew it would take both of his arms to lift her down from the wagon.

"Never you mind," she firmly told him. She abruptly got up off the bench, snatched up her carpetbag, and thrust it into his reaching arms. "Now turn around."

"Why? You think I've never seen a girl's petticoats?"

"Mine you haven't. And you never will."

"Well, pardon me, Your Highness." And he gave her a royal bow before heading for the cabin with her carpetbag.

Drew had taken only a few long strides when he suddenly stopped at the unmistakable sound of ripping fabric. Slowly, he set Marnette's bag down on the footpath and just as slowly turned around. Grinning.

Marnette knew she must look ridiculous: one leg in and one leg out of the wagon—like a runaway rag doll caught in the act.

And as Drew Britton slowly walked back to the wagon, she wished he would have come right out and laughed. That would have been easier to bear than that smug masculine grin, telling Marnette Coulter how wrong she had been about his never seeing her petticoats. And that, with them so firmly caught on a spike, he was seeing even more.

It was maddening, the way he took his sweet time freeing the tangled lace from the big nail and setting her down once she had slipped into his arms.

"Yes, sir," he told himself. "Pretty as a little china doll."

And to this day—even as the town's sack-frocked temporary schoolmarm of nearly twenty—Marnette still wondered what might have happened if Doc Britton had not come out of the cabin just then.

Whether Drew Britton would have dared to kiss her.

And what she would have done if he had.

four

Having dismissed her students for the summer and stowed everything away for September, Marnette started on her final task: that of closing the six schoolhouse windows.

She had already been aware of the lull in all the racket outside and could now see that the town hall builders had stopped working to eat their lunches in the shade of one of the schoolyard trees. All the more reason for her to leave by the back door and take the long way home through the woods—just one more maneuver in her avoidance of Drew Britton the past three years.

Part of her ongoing strategy was going into town only when absolutely necessary—when she needed to buy some thread or fabric at the trading post. Another thing was never going with her cousin Emilie to any of Abbie Britton's monthly sewing bees. Yet another was trying to stay healthy, so she would never need to make a sick call at Doc Britton's cabin.

But there was no way Ina Coulter's granddaughter could escape going to church on Sunday. And though Marnette yawned through the last half of the Reverend Humphries' long, drawn-out sermon, she always dreaded the end of the service because the Coulters and the Brittons, long-time friends, always lingered outside the church for a short visit. And Drew Britton always took part in the little Sunday morning reunion.

Though Marnette sometimes joined Emilie in chatting with Abbie Britton and her half sister, Wilting Sunflower, she carefully avoided any talk, or even any eye contact, with Abbie's twin brother. And she always pretended not to have heard any of his comments, especially those after she had become the temporary schoolmarm: such as the ongoing wager among the old-timers at the trading post, as to how long it might be before there were curtains on the schoolhouse windows...and the younger men wondering if there was an age limit on boys allowed to attend school.

Closing the last of those curtainless windows on this last day of school, Marnette dared not look too long at those over-aged and bare-chested "schoolboys" eating their lunches under one of the schoolyard trees. If she had, she might have seen that one of them was truant. And when she left the schoolhouse by its back door, she might not have been so surprised to find Drew Britton lounging against the backyard well.

"My! If it isn't the old schoolmarm."

In her startled but quickly withdrawn glance at him, Marnette saw that he had gotten back into his blue workday shirt and apparently had doused his sun-scorched head at the well.

As for his greeting, she was sure the doctor's son was telling the temporary schoolmarm he was not the least bit discouraged by all her old-maidish trappings. No more than he was by this latest attempt at avoiding him: going out the back door and taking the long way home.

Her only defense against that was heading for the woods as if she had neither seen nor heard him.

"Hold on there a second, Marnie."

His further shortening of her name—as if they might have been on the most intimate of terms these past three years—was something more than a surprise. But Marnette recovered quickly enough to tell him, over her shoulder, "I don't have a second." Perhaps her first words to Drew Britton since the day they had met. "I need to get home right away."

"Going through the woods?"

Marnette felt a sudden flush, for they both knew that going through the woods added at least ten more minutes to her already long walk home.

"It's cooler going through the woods," she told him as, with several long-legged strides, he was soon walking beside her.

"True," he nodded. "But it can sometimes be dangerous for a girl to walk alone through the woods."

You ought to know, Marnette thought, catching herself before actually saying it. She already had a long list of lies to account for, but she would never be guilty of sarcasm—not when she herself had suffered the sting of unkind words.

Besides, she didn't want to admit that she knew anything—or ever cared to know anything—about Drew Britton's past.

❧

If, in leaving Boston, she had thought she was turning her back on the specter of death, Marnette had had a most rude awakening on her arrival in Chappie Creek. Despite all its signs of life, the town seemed surrounded by death—especially with Massacre Hill and all its grim gravestones brooding over the prairie settlement.

Even if one did not count the massacre of over twenty years ago, death had stalked almost every cabin in town. Twelve years ago it had presided over the birth of the last Coulter baby, making a young widower of Thad Coulter and leaving Ina Coulter both mother and grandmother to his three young children.

Doc Britton, too, had had more than his share of untimely death. First, his young Indian wife had died, almost twenty-five years ago. Then, some years later, a stillborn baby, followed by the death of that baby's mother—the doctor's second wife—mysteriously on a cold winter's night. Though people still talked about the way Jessica Britton had died, Marnette was never able to get the whole, or even the same, story on it.

The story she did know—as did everyone in Chappie Creek—was the one about Drew Britton: how he had killed a man six years ago, one morning out in the woods.

Someone had even made up a song about it, and whenever she heard that song—and hardly a week went by that she didn't

—Marnette would cringe.

> *'Twas in the woods*
> *At early morn,*
> *A brand new day*
> *Just barely born;*
>
> *Most Chappie Creek*
> *Folks still abed,*
> *Young Drew shot*
> *Crazy Otis dead!*

The first time she had heard the song, a few days after her surprise arrival by stagecoach, Marnette had not paid too much attention to it—mostly because it reminded her of some of those bawdy sailor's songs her father used to sing before he was totally drunk.

Because it sounded to her like "Young Droo," she thought the children might be singing about some mythical Chinaman. It did not become "Drew" in her mind, and she did not connect it with "Britton" until she noticed how the younger boys in town—and more especially her own two cousins, Theodore and Robert—gaped in barefaced hero worship whenever the doctor's son walked by.

Having resolved to avoid Drew Britton from the very start, the last thing Marnette Coulter would have done was ask any questions about him. Thus, the story behind the children's song had come to her in bits and pieces, most of them in eavesdropping on the older menfolks' jawing around the potbellied stove the few times she had gone to the trading post. Indeed, it seemed to be one of their favorite stories: how Otis Grimes had met his fate. And whenever they first mentioned his name, they would always tap their foreheads—meaning, of course, that Otis had been "touched," or out of his mind.

He had gotten that way, the story went, after his wife and baby had been butchered—along with all those other unsuspecting Chappie Creek folks—that terrible summer day when a band of drunken Indians had swooped down on them from what was now known as Massacre Hill.

What most folks had not known—until he himself was dead—was that Otis Grimes had been the one who had traded the applejack to those once friendly Indians.

But Ina Coulter had somehow known. And she was sure that was what had driven the brandy-guzzling trapper out of his mind: the knowledge that he himself had killed his wife and baby.

However she had gotten her knowledge—by some mysterious Indian intuition or from Otis himself—Ina Coulter had kept it to herself, for fear the other menfolks might seize Otis and lynch him. Vengeance, she firmly believed, was in the hands of the Lord. At the same time, Ina feared the guilt-ridden trapper might someday go on the warpath himself and kill some innocent Indian.

Ina Coulter had been right. But it had taken all of fifteen brandy-swilling years for Otis Grimes to finally go berserk. And when he did, his victim not only was innocent, but was also only half Indian.

He had been waiting for Wilting Sunflower one morning in the woods. But someone else had been up early that morning, hunting in those same woods. And when sixteen-year-old Drew Britton fired the day's first shot, it had been into the skull of Otis Grimes, caught in the act of ravaging Drew's half-Indian sister, her ankle caught in a bear trap.

And that was how "The Ballad of Young Drew" had been born: a song still sung by the Chappie Creek children at play— even the little girls when they skipped rope in the schoolyard.

Marnette never ceased to be shocked at such an open celebration of murder, especially when most of the townsfolk considered themselves good Christians.

But she knew there was at least one person in town who did not celebrate the death of Otis Grimes. Someone who mourned his passing enough to place a small bouquet of violets on his grave every spring.

૨૦

Coming to the schoolhouse that morning, Marnette had marveled at the many flowers abloom in the woods. Now, on her walk home through those same woods, she was aware of only one thing: Drew Britton, walking beside her. And the excuse she had given him for taking the long way home—that it was cooler in the woods.

"And you'd be cooler yet," he said with a nod at her high-collared dress, "if you opened the top of that gunny sack."

Marnette opened her mouth and then quickly closed it. For her to be shocked, or even pretend to be shocked, at his reference to any part of her dress would be ridiculous. Especially when Drew Britton already knew so much about Marnette Coulter's underpinnings.

"And let someone carry this bag for you," he added, taking the clumsy carpetbag from her.

This time she was sorry she hadn't objected. She felt totally defenseless without the big bag, as if it might have been a bulwark between her and her so-long-avoided escort.

"That must be a whale of a lunch you have in here," he said, shifting the bag to his other hand.

"It isn't only my lunch," she said simply. He didn't have to know about those two bricks—or those three cherished books from Stuart Whittington. Indeed, she never intended that Drew Britton should know anything about her—more especially what might or might not please her.

But he didn't know this. And even if he did, he might still have asked her. "And what do you think of our illustrious town hall?"

She glanced backward, but could see nothing now of the slowly rising red-brick building. She never once looked at it through the schoolhouse window that she did not think of Stuart Whittington. Not only had a town hall been his idea to begin with, he had helped design the building—much on the same order as Independence Hall in Philadelphia, where he had been born and had studied.

"It would take more than a fancy brick town hall to turn Chappie Creek into another Philadelphia," she told Drew Britton and maybe Stuart Whittington, too. "Or Boston," she added, thinking how much she would hate it, if it did.

She was not sure just when she had come to love the crude prairie town and its surrounding countryside. But no matter when it was, she was not about to admit something so personal to Drew Britton.

"Boston," he said dourly, as if he might have heard of that seaboard city once too often. "What's so special about Boston?"

"For one thing," she said, lifting her skirt to step over a fallen log, "it's civilized."

Drew was silent a moment, as if digesting that. Marnette herself was having some trouble reconciling her claim with what she remembered—or would rather not remember—about some of the "civilized" people back east.

"Even Boston probably began with log cabins," Drew argued.

"I mean its customs." She quickly dropped the hem of her skirt. "In Boston," she told him, "you wouldn't find men working without any shirts on."

"Maybe so," he said dryly. "But I had the notion there were some young ladies in this town who didn't too much mind it."

Marnette was glad she had to duck her head to avoid a low-hanging branch so Drew couldn't see her face. She was sure he was telling her that he had seen her, with her spelling book, at the schoolhouse window.

And though she had not yet given him a second glance since finding him at the well, Marnette was sorely aware of how he looked now: his flaxen hair still damp from its dousing and his blue shirt only half buttoned over his previously bare chest.

He and Tim Piper were two of the few beardless men in town. Marnette had no idea why the miller's son would want to go to all the bother of shaving each day, but she suspected the doctor's son was fearful whiskers would hide the small hollow in his right cheek that always turned into an eye-catching dimple when he smiled.

But nothing could have hidden the arrogant lift of his chin, or that knowing look in his green tomcat's eyes—as if Drew Britton was sure there were any number of Chappie Creek women who wouldn't mind seeing him without a shirt.

They now came to a small clearing in the woods—the little peaceful forest glade where her grandmother sometimes came to pray. Only yesterday Marnette had herded her twelve students into the cool and shady glade to eat their lunch. Right now her own stomach was begging for today's uneaten lunch, still in her bag.

"By the way," Drew said, as if reading her mind, "might there possibly be enough lunch for two?"

She knew what he was suggesting: that they should stop in the clearing and share her lunch.

"Not really," she told him. Two corn muffins and an apple were barely enough for a self-retired schoolmarm, much less a temporarily idle town hall builder. Besides, she was sure he had his own lunch waiting for him back under the schoolyard tree. And surely, he did not intend to walk her all the way home.

Whatever had been Drew Britton's intentions, it seemed that now he decided to take himself a little break—with or without any lunch. For he suddenly sat down on a fallen log with her carpetbag between his feet.

Outside of wresting the bag from him, there was nothing for Marnette to do but sit down beside him. She couldn't help noticing his fingers, spread open on his denim knees: long, slender fingers, just like his father's. Except that Doc Britton's hands were never sunburned or calloused.

Though she wouldn't have admitted it, not even to herself, Marnette was not the only one in town who wondered at the doctor's son having never gone east to study doctoring himself. That Drew Britton, still living at home, was content to earn his keep by doing odd jobs in town—the latest being one of the builders of the new town hall—was a puzzle to them all.

Yet Marnette did know, from idle talk at the trading post, that even as a boy, Drew had shown little interest in his father's profession. And when he had not been out in the woods, hunting with his rifle, he had been roaming those same woods in search of wood for whittling.

After Cyrus Gage had come to town and set up his sawmill beside the creek, the doctor's teenage son had simply changed his wood-hunting grounds to Gage's mill yard, finding even better pieces of discarded wood to be used in his favorite pastime: sitting on the trading post steps and whittling. This often resulted in little carved wooden animals—and sometimes people—which he would then present to one or more of the restless children also sitting on the steps while their parents were inside, loading up on supplies.

While most folks in town had considered it an idle boy's folly, Cyrus Gage had been quick to spot in Drew Britton's wood-carving a marketable talent. And before long he had expanded his mill operations to include a small woodworking shop wherein the doctor's son could carve to his heart's content on handmade furniture ordered by his fellow townsfolk.

But most Chappie Creek families had brought their own furniture from back East, and Drew had ended up doing odd jobs for those families: mending broken table legs and replacing weather-worn window frames or boot-worn cabin thresholds. And, when necessary, he carved a new wooden or stone grave marker for Massacre Hill.

Marnette did not know if Drew Britton had carved the stone that marked Otis Grimes' neglected grave on the hill, but she shuddered, even now, to think that he might have.

❧

If she had thought her unwelcome escort had given up hoping to share her lunch, Marnette was wrong. For it was not long after she had sat down beside him on the fallen log that he opened her carpetbag and reached inside. But it was not her lunch pail that he first lifted out. It was the pearl-handled mirror she had earlier looked into at the schoolhouse, bemoaning her failure at looking frumpy and spinsterish.

"From the pastor's wife," she quickly told him. As if cherishing the mirror as a keepsake from Sarah Humphries—and not feminine vanity—was the reason she carried it in her bag. She thought the matching pearl-handled hairbrush would be next out of the bag, but Drew was now holding up one of her also-cherished books from Boston.

"Well, now—what have we here?"

Marnette quickly snatched the book from him: the elegant leather-bound volume of poems by John Keats. "You wouldn't be interested in this."

"Of course not," he agreed. "None of us prairie town barbarians know how to read."

She gave him a sharp glance. "I never said that."

"But you may as well have."

That was enough to close her mouth. Indeed, she found it hard to believe she was having this conversation—was actually arguing—with the man she had so carefully avoided the past three years.

Again fishing into her bag, he came up with the other two

books from Stuart Whittington, almost as if he had expected to
find more.

"*The Compleat Works of William Shakespeare,*" he read from
the cover of the first book. And then the second: " and *Charles
and Mary Lamb.*" He made them sound like some rare species
of flower never before found out on the prairie.

And were they not? Indeed, the only books some Chappie
Creek families ever laid their hands on were the dog-eared
hymnals in church and their own worn-out Bibles at home.

"And where might these rare gems have come from?" he
asked her.

"Stuart Whittington," she told him, snatching the last two
books from him.

"Really?" She thought she heard a tinge of doubt in his tone,
as if he, too, might find such a romantic, literary choice by the
stuffy schoolmaster somewhat hard to believe. "And you've
had the time to read them?"

"Every night," she said, hugging the three rescued volumes
to her breast. "The very last thing I do before getting into bed."

She was immediately sorry she had said that, told Drew
Britton something as intimate as that. Especially when she
had gone to so much trouble, all these years, never to talk to
him.

"But could there be one night," he asked her, "that you'd be
willing to do something else?"

She was not about to answer that.

"Such as going with a man to the Founders' Day ball?"

Though he had only said "a man," Marnette was sure he
meant himself. And she hoped he didn't notice the little tremor
in her hands as she slipped the three books back into the carpetbag. But hadn't she known, the very day they had met, that
this would someday happen? Still, she was momentarily speech-
less at Drew Britton's offhand offer to escort her to the August
ball at the new town hall and her mind raced in search of a

believable rebuff.

She found it among the three cherished books, now safely back in her bag. "I've already promised to go with a certain gentleman."

"And just who might that be?" As if surprised that Marnette Coulter might think there were any gentlemen in Chappie Creek.

"Mister Whittington."

"Old Muttonchops?" This time there was more than a trace of doubt in Drew Britton's voice. In fact, he all but laughed.

There were many in town who would have come right out and laughed, to think of the so stodgy and staid bachelor schoolmaster kicking up his heels at the Founders' Day ball. Marnette herself might at least have smiled, had the lie not been so necessary in rebuffing Drew Britton.

"What makes you think he'll be back by then?" Drew challenged.

"I don't merely think it—I know it."

She was certain that, despite his long and letterless absence, the schoolmaster would be back from Boston in time for the dedication of the new town hall. After all, it had been his brainchild to begin with. And as for escorting anyone to the ball, who else but the one who had so willingly filled his shoes at the schoolhouse while he was gone?

Convinced by her own logic, Marnette confidently got up from the fallen log. But when she attempted to retrieve her carpetbag, Drew lay his hand on hers.

"Know he'll be back? How do you know that?"

His green eyes were so intent on hers that she felt the need to back up her logic. Even if it meant telling another lie. "From the note he sent with the last book."

While she inwardly squirmed at the lie, she felt totally safe with it. For though it was true that no one in Chappie Creek ever got a letter or a package that everyone else in town did not know it, it was possible that a paper-wrapped book from Boston might also contain a small hand-written note.

"Well," Drew loudly sighed. "A promise is a promise." And when she picked up her carpetbag and headed for the trees, he made no attempt to stop her.

But all the way home, Marnette was haunted by the quickening of her pulse at finding him behind the schoolhouse. And how it had quickened again at the touch of his warm, work-roughened hand.

Nor could she shake the feeling that Drew Britton did not believe any one of the lies she had told him about Stuart Whittington.

five

Cradling a tin of hot biscuits in a folded flour-sack towel, Marnette almost dropped it on her short trip from the hearth to the breakfast table.

"What's ailing you?" her grandmother asked without turning from her task of frying bacon.

Though Marnette had learned to laugh at the notion that her half-Indian grandmother might have unearthly powers, she sometimes thought the little woman had eyes in the back of her head.

"Another bad dream?" her grandmother now asked.

Marnette pretended not to have heard. She was not about to confess to anyone, not even herself, what was making her so jittery and butter-fingered this morning: the sleep she had lost last night, reliving her lie-loaded encounter with Drew Britton.

"Well, if it was a nightmare," said her cousin Emilie, busy pouring cups of thick buttermilk, "that's the first one I ever slept through."

The very first night that Emilie Coulter had had a partner in her canopied bed, she had been awakened by her cousin's nightmarish scream—an all too frequent happening that had earned Marnette a room to herself on the dormitory floor back at the Boston boarding school.

Only after she had been with her new family for almost a year had her nightmares become less frequent. Indeed, she only had them, now, after a trip to the trading post—and after getting a whiff of Trader Farnsworth's whiskey-loaded breath.

While her scream always woke Emilie, at least her grandmother—who had her own added-on bedroom in the back of

43

her son's cabin—no longer came rushing into the room. Though in the morning, she would again urge Marnette to talk out her disturbing dreams, drawing on the handed-down wisdom of her tribal ancestors: that it was unhealthy for anyone to harbor too many untold dreams.

❧

But Marnette knew she could never tell her grandmother the substance of her dreams, not without hurting the tiny outspoken woman she had come to love.

The day she had arrived in Chappie Creek, Marnette would not have believed there could ever be anything that might break the heart of the small, half-Indian woman who was her paternal grandmother. Even today it was sometimes hard to believe. Especially when Ina Coulter was "looking Indian," as her family described a certain mysterious, somewhat stony expression that would sometimes steal over her face.

It was with that same stony look that the little woman had, three years ago, greeted her orphaned granddaughter and the news that her long-lost son, Thomas, was dead. She had said not a word to Marnette before picking up her woven shawl and walking out of the cabin.

Marnette had wanted to die right there on the braided fireside rug. Had she traveled halfway across the world, only to again be rejected by a grandmother?

It was Doc Britton, familiar with the ways of Indians, who had put her mind at ease. Her grandmother, he told her, had gone to Massacre Hill—the place of the dead—to privately mourn for her son.

Even today there were some folks who harkened back to that day as "the day of Ina's wailing," claiming they had been able to hear Ina Coulter's grieving as far off as Piper's gristmill.

When she returned to the cabin an hour later, Ina Coulter still did not embrace her dead son's child. She merely glanced at Marnette, seated on a bench with her carpetbag at her feet, and told her other granddaughter, Emilie, to "set another place at the table."

It was not until that night—when the family awoke to her nightmarish scream—that Marnette first felt her prairie grandmother's arms around her and heard the maternal softness in her voice.

"It's all right, dearie, Grandma's going to take good care of you."

And because she had come to love the shrewd and sometimes stoic little "squaw" who still sometimes stole off to Massacre Hill, Marnette had vowed never to tell her the truth: all that had happened in the many years that Ina's youngest son, Thomas, had been missing.

She sometimes wondered, though, if her widowed grandmother had not known that Tommy Coulter, even at the tender age of twenty-one, had already grown overly fond of whiskey. And that the night in Boston, when he had been shanghaied as one of a sea-bound ship's crew, he already had been drunk as a shore-leave sailor.

When five years had passed without any word from her youngest son, Ina Coulter had packed up and taken the next wagon train west to live with her oldest son, Thaddeus, who had earlier gone west with his bride to settle a homestead somewhere out on the prairie and the fate of Thomas Coulter had remained a mystery until the miraculous appearance, three years ago, of his suddenly orphaned daughter.

Marnette still refused to shed any further light on the mystery, convinced that what her grandmother didn't know could never hurt her. Why should she tell Ina Coulter that the spray of salt water had done nothing to curb her sailor son's craving for whiskey, or just how mean and ugly all that whiskey had finally made Thomas Coulter? Or that the always drunk, always brawling seaman was eventually suspected of having killed a fellow shipmate?

Finally, not even the most nefarious of sea captains would take him on as part of his crew, and Tommy Coulter had joined another kind of crew: working on the river as a logger. That was when he had met Marnette's mother.

To this day, Marnette could not imagine her parents ever having been in love. And because she had been born into it, she had not known as a young child that other families did not live that way: all that shouting and all those screams, over the years steadily growing worse—each night her father came home drunk being worse than the night before. Until it seemed the only end to her and her mother's misery might be his killing them both.

But it was her father who had that fatal accident on the river: a fight with one of his fellow loggers in which Tommy Coulter—in no shape to either fight or swim—had fallen into the churning water and drowned.

And that had been the first time, in all of her ten years, that Marnette had heard so much as a hint from her mother that there might be a God: some unseen, benevolent Being who had finally heard all of Cynthia Coulter's silent pleas and had mercifully put an end to her and Marnette's nightly suffering.

But that was before she and her mother had stood on the steps of the big stone Boston church and Marnette had felt the wrath of her maternal grandmother's God. Before those last, six, prison-like years at the boarding school that had ended with her mother's own fatal accident.

The heaviest thing Marnette Coulter had carried to Chappie Creek on that stagecoach three years ago had been a heart full of bitter memories—the strongest being that of a small, frightened child trembling under the covers at the sound of her father savagely beating her mother. Choking back her own screams, lest her father might hear them and come into the bedroom to vent his drunken fury on her, as well. Screams that came out, now, in all of her nightmarish dreams.

"No! Please, Papa—no!"

❧

Though last night she had been spared one of those terrible dreams, Marnette still had not had the best night's sleep, twisting and turning beside her cousin Emilie for several hours: angry with herself for having lied to Drew Britton. Even angrier that the lie had been so flimsy.

The truth was that, though she had agreed to make six other women's gowns, Marnette had no intention of going herself to the Founders' Day ball in August, with or without an escort. And there was no reason in the world why she shouldn't have simply told Drew Britton that.

She now went back to the hearth for the platter of fried bacon her grandmother had finally declared done, glad that this time her hands were somewhat steadier.

"Go call up the ladder," her grandmother then told her, "and tell those two slug-a-beds up there to get hustling."

She meant Marnette's other two cousins, Emilie's younger brothers, Theodore and Robert, still up in the loft where they slept with their father.

"And if they know what's good for them, they'll be down before their father comes in from the well."

six

Only moments before their father came in from his morning wash-up at the backyard well did Theodore and Robert scramble down from the loft—complaining, as usual, at having to get up before the birds.

Being the town's foremost wheat farmer, Thad Coulter never waited for the birds. Nor did he allow his field-hand sons that privilege. And because he always expected a hearty breakfast of hot biscuits and bacon before starting any day, winter or summer, the women in his household had to be up even earlier.

This was one of the rare mornings that the biscuits had made it to the table before Thad Coulter. And Marnette knew why. Last night had been the special closed meeting of the town council at the schoolhouse, and when she and the rest of the family had gone to bed, her uncle had not yet come home.

When her uncle finally came in from the well, Marnette felt a surge of warm regard (she was not yet ready to call it love) for this blustery, bearded man who was so blessedly different from his brother, Thomas.

Though he, too, had lost several hours of sleep, Marnette thought his eyes were unusually bright this morning as he rubbed his callused farmer's palms together before sitting down at the table. And the way he so quickly said grace, she was sure Thaddeus Coulter was bursting with some important news.

He said nothing, though, until he had broken open one of the plump buttermilk biscuits and spread its two steaming halves with thick golden honey. And when he spoke directly to her, Marnette was sure that what he told her was not yet his big news.

"By the way, Marnie, there was a package for you on the schoolhouse steps." He nodded toward the fireplace. "I set it up there, on the mantel."

Glancing toward the hearth, only now did Marnette see the small brown paper parcel beside one of the pewter plates on the fireplace mantel. For the first time, she was not thrilled at the prospect of yet another expensive book from Stuart Whittington, for this one could only mean the schoolmaster was not yet on his way back from Boston, making her lie to Drew Britton all the more flimsy.

"From her secret admirer," said fifteen-year-old Theodore, batting his eyelids and causing a twitter of laughter around the table—from all but Marnette.

In Chappie Creek, to accept a gift from any unmarried man was as good as accepting his proposal of marriage. Probably the only two exceptions to this rule were the Reverend Richard Humphries and Stuart Whittington. Indeed, it was because he was so stiff and stuffy that Marnette had felt so safe in her friendship with the bachelor schoolmaster.

"It's no secret," she told her breakfasting family. "And he's no admirer."

"I surely hope not," said her grandmother. "Half again your age—and a heathen besides."

While Ina Coulter reluctantly gave the unmarried schoolmaster his due, both as a scholar and a gentleman, she also counted him among the dozen or so lost souls in Chappie Creek who never went to church on Sunday.

"A girl could do worse than marry an older man, Grandma," said Emilie, seated beside Marnette at the table.

Marnette wondered if her cousin might not be speaking in her own defense. Or was she just imagining that Emilie's face always seemed flushed whenever Doc Britton came to the cabin?

Whatever, no one had to ask what Emilie meant by there being something worse than a girl's marrying an older man:

becoming a burden to her family as an "old maid." Apparently Ina Coulter was in agreement, for it was one of the rare times she had no answer for someone at the table.

But Marnette knew there was something infinitely worse than being an old maid. And though she had lost some sleep over it, this morning she was even firmer in her resolve that no man would ever claim Marnette Coulter as his wife. Least of all, a man who had already killed someone.

As if to set a seal on her renewed resolve, Marnette spread her yet untouched biscuit with honey and took a healthy bite.

"And there's something else I should tell you," said her uncle.

"Yes?" Had someone on the town council heard from the schoolmaster? A letter telling of his imminent return?

"You know the Founders' Day ball?" said her uncle. As if it might be necessary to refresh the memory of Chappie Creek's busy gown-sewing seamstress.

Marnette nodded.

"Well, the council voted—"

"To cancel it?" croaked her cousin Emilie. She was more than halfway through making her own elaborate gown for the upcoming ball. With the fervor, Marnette thought, of a young woman with definite designs as to which of the evening's un-attached men might find her irresistible as a dancing partner.

"No, of course not," said Thad Coulter. "But the men—it was their womenfolk who put them up to it—decided there should be something special for the youngsters that day."

"Fireworks?" said twelve-year-old Robert, suddenly awake over his breakfast plate.

"No," his father chuckled. "The ladies had something a bit quieter in mind. A pageant or some such thing."

Each of his sons gave out a disappointed groan.

"That's a lovely idea," said Emilie. Her grandmother, busy spreading a biscuit, also nodded her approval.

"I was sure you ladies would agree," said Thad Coulter. "So

I told them Marnette, here, would be only too happy to take charge of it—what with school being over and all this free time on her hands."

He reached for another biscuit as if to reward himself for having so neatly solved the problem of his niece's free time. He paused in the biscuit's breaking to glance over at her.

"What's the matter, Marnie—you look as if you just swallowed a bee hive."

"Too much honey," she said, taking a long sip of her buttermilk. It was not the sweet syrupy honey she had almost choked on, but her barely suppressed cry of dismay. With all those ball gowns to be finished before Founders' Day—and all her regular chores at the cabin—where was she to find the time to take charge of any children's pageant?

"And that's all you deep thinkers decided?" her grandmother asked. "To hold a children's show?" Everyone in town knew the council had called their special meeting last night to make some important appointments.

"No," her son smiled, and the news-telling gleam was back in his dark eyes. But only after he had spread the two halves of his second buttermilk biscuit with honey did he focus his eyes on his two sons.

"And come Monday, you lads'll really have to watch your step—really have to mind your P's and Q's."

It was an admonishment used even back in Boston, but Marnette had found no one in either place who could tell her exactly what the two letters stood for.

She also thought it might have made more sense if her uncle had been warning the Widow Jaster's two oldest boys rather than his own mildly mischievous sons. And then, noting the mischief in his eyes, she was sure her uncle was merely teasing them.

"We now have an official town constable to keep an eye on all you young scalawags."

"Oh," said Theodore, anything but overjoyed at learning he might have another watchdog in his life. He already had three: his father, his grandmother, and his older sister.

But his brother, Robert, obligingly asked their father, "Who?"

"Guess," he said, plopping the biscuit into his mouth.

"Surely not Tim Piper," said Emilie.

Her own mouth half full of biscuit, Marnette silently echoed Emilie's hope. She just couldn't see Tim Piper, one of the town's few real gentlemen, stalking the town with a rifle over his shoulder.

"No," her uncle shook his dark head, "but we did appoint Tim Piper as town clerk."

Marnette murmured her approval. A partner with his father at the town's gristmill, Tim Piper was known to have a good head for figures. He was also honest as the day was long.

"An excellent choice," said Emilie.

"So is the one for town constable," said her father. "And I'm surprised none of you has guessed."

"Homer Farnsworth," said Theodore, sending another ripple of laughter around the table. Not only was Homer known as the town's chief purveyor of gossip and for his frequent "medicinal" use of mail-ordered whiskey, the trader's eyesight was so bad that he sometimes mistook sugar for flour and rifle shot for peppercorns. Hardly someone to keep an eye on things in town.

"What we need a town constable for is beyond me," said Marnette's grandmother, passing the rasher of bacon to her farmer son. "A community of solid, God-fearing, church-going Christians—"

"Not everybody goes to church, Ma," Thad reminded her, taking several strips of the crisp bacon. "And even some of our regular Sunday churchgoers step out of line every now and then."

"Only those who let their cider go hard."

Everyone in town knew Ina Coulter's thoughts on the evil of drinking anything stronger than buttermilk—a bit of local lore that had given Marnette Coulter no small amount of comfort after her arrival in Chappie Creek.

"I'll wager half the souls in the down-under have applejack on their breath," said her grandmother.

"There's only one way you could win that wager, Ma," chuckled her son, "and that's to go down there and see for yourself."

"Hmph!" said Ina Coulter, another of the rare times she could not think of anything else to say.

"Anyway," said Marnette's uncle, "like it or not, Chappie Creek has itself an official peace officer."

"For goodness sake—who?" demanded Emilie, as if suddenly weary of her father's little breakfast table guessing game.

"Who *would* the council choose," he asked no one in particular, "but the best shot in town?"

"Drew Britton!" his two sons loudly chorused.

"Right you are," nodded their father.

And once again Marnette had trouble swallowing her mouthful of biscuit.

"Could it be you don't approve of the council's choice?" asked her uncle.

"Hardly," she said after another relieving sip of buttermilk.

"Why?" asked Emilie, beside her.

Marnette didn't answer. She didn't think she had to.

"You mean what happened in the woods?" said Emilie.

Marnette's continued silence was her answer.

"Oh, for goodness sake!" snorted her cousin. "That's ancient history."

"And he was only a boy," added her father.

Marnette did not say what she was thinking: that Drew Britton had been all of sixteen when he had killed Otis Grimes. And that Thad Coulter himself was always telling his sons—neither of them yet sixteen—that now that they were men, he expected them to work like men.

"Besides," demanded Emilie, "what do you think he should have done—let him kill her besides?" She did not say the forbidden word, never spoken in all the whisperings behind Wilting Sunflower's back.

And again Marnette did not say what she was thinking: that there were some women in town who thought death might have been the more merciful outcome for Doc Britton's firstborn daughter. It was bad enough that she was half Indian, but to have lost her virtue as well—there wasn't a man in Chappie Creek who would consider taking her as his wife.

Neither did Marnette speak the other thought in her mind: that there were at least seven men in town—her uncle included—who might also be a bit touched in the head. She could not believe anyone sound of mind—however young Drew Britton may have been—would choose as a town's official keeper of law and order a man guilty of murder himself.

"And what does Doc Britton think about it?" asked Ina Coulter, a more than curious question, since the town's doctor was also on the town council.

"Well, of course, Clay abstained from voting for his own son," said Marnette's uncle. "Though I'm sure he long ago stopped hoping the lad would want to put an M.D. at the end of his name."

"Which means," said his mother, "that he can chuck any hopes he might have had to take down his shingle and retire soon."

"He's not anywhere near old enough to retire," said Emilie, almost angrily.

Surer now about her cousin and the town's handsome widowed doctor, Marnette wondered if she shouldn't someday tell Emilie what she herself had learned about the doctor three years ago, seated at another table in a place called Trapper's Bend: *I've already put two wives in an early grave—I wouldn't chance making it three.*

"And anyway," said Thad Coulter, "the whole town knows where Drew Britton's talent lies." He nodded at the cherry hutch in the corner, made by the town's handiest cabinetmaker.

"Then why in the world would he want to take on the job as town constable?" asked Ina.

"He didn't, at first. Not until we promised him he wouldn't have to carry a gun."

Theodore and Robert exchanged crestfallen looks at this bit of news.

"And the added income was the clincher," said their father. "In fact, Doc Britton said that's the only thing that's kept the lad from marrying—not making enough at odd jobs to support himself and a wife."

"Well, that certainly will be good news to a whole lot of young ladies in town," said Ina Coulter, "that Drew Britton is finally ready to get married."

Her grandsons again traded gloomy glances. This was even worse news: that their gunless hero would want to do something as dumb as getting married.

"Bad news for most of those young ladies," said their father, reaching for his flour-sack napkin. "The doc says Drew's already been secretly courting his future wife."

"Really?" said Emilie. "Who?"

"He wouldn't say." He wiped his mouth with the napkin, signaling the end of both his news sharing and his breakfast. "But he did say that everyone will know who—when Drew takes her home from the Founders' Day ball."

This time Marnette did choke. So badly that Emilie had to whack her on the back.

seven

Sunday began as anything but a day of rest at the Coulter cabin, since the farmer and his family had to be up even earlier to get their morning chores done before climbing into the buckboard for the ten o'clock worship service at the church.

As they pulled into the churchyard, Marnette thought that, if ever there were a small miracle in Chappie Creek, it was the way in which the white frame building—a schoolhouse and meeting hall during the week—became the town's church on Sunday.

Yet she knew what caused the sudden change: the Sunday-best clothes worn by the congregation and the "Praise-the-Lord" look on some of their faces as they walked up the steps.

She herself never walked up the steps of the Chappie Creek church that she did not think of that Sunday, ten years ago, on the steps of the big stone church in Boston—the first and last time she had seen her other grandmother.

When her father had drowned, Marnette had felt something almost akin to joy in her nine-year-old heart, knowing she no longer had to fear his footsteps on the stairs. But it was only a matter of weeks before she found herself close to wishing her father had not perished in the churning river. At least when Thomas Coulter had staggered home drunk, with what little was left of his logger's pay, there had been coal for the stove and food on the table.

Not that her mother had not tried to find some work. But so physically weakened from all those years of abuse, Cynthia Coulter was not strong enough for the only jobs that were available for women: housecleaning and laundering for well-to-do ladies in the better part of town.

When they had not eaten in two days, Marnette's mother had taken her by the hand and gone back to that part of town: this time to her own widowed and well-to-do mother's big Victorian house. Only to have the hired housekeeper shut the door in their faces.

For Cynthia Coulter, née Adams, had been declared dead by her mother even before Marnette had been born—no matter that she had covered her sin by marrying the muckworm. And perhaps that was an even greater sin: that the daughter of Bedelia Adams, a direct descendant of those who had come over on the Mayflower, had chosen to give herself to a scurvy logger of such dubious birth.

But Cynthia Coulter was desperate. And in the hope that the sight of her innocent and impoverished granddaughter—on the steps of the church and on the Lord's Day—would soften Bedelia Adams' heart, Marnette's mother had waited one Sunday for the service to end and for her mother to come down the steps in her Sunday best.

But it seemed the dissolute daughter was to commit her greatest sin yet: asking her mother for help in sight of all those other good Christian pillars of the big stone church.

"Not for me, Mamma—for the child," Marnette's mother had begged her. "Just look at her, and you can see she's not had enough to eat."

But Bedelia Adams did not lower herself to look at her only grandchild who had been conceived in sin with a man whose blood was anything but pure Boston blue.

"You can *both* starve," she hissed with self-righteous venom. "and the sooner the better!"

But they hadn't starved. That night Marnette's mother left her alone in their shabby apartment, and when she came home in the morning, there was breakfast on the table.

Then it became a regular thing: Marnette's mother going out alone every night and coming home in the morning with a sack of food.

When she went out in the evening, Cynthia Coulter did not look at all like a young penniless widow, but rather like a painted shop window mannequin. She did something different to her hair, too, and for the first time in her life, Marnette saw rings in her mother's ears and bracelets on her wrists. Even the clothes she wore were different—each tight-fitting bodice cut lower than the one before.

When her mother began bringing strange men home with her, there would be curious sounds from the other bedroom, and once in a while even a soft laugh from her mother. Though Marnette did not understand those sounds, there was no one in the world who could have made her believe there was anything wrong in her mother's bringing men into her bedroom who were able to make her laugh. Especially when it somehow also meant food on the table and coal in the stove and even prettier dresses for her still young and pretty mother.

One morning, shortly after Marnette's tenth birthday, her mother told her she was going into business in another part of town, and that she had made special arrangements for Marnette, too. That afternoon she had taken Marnette in a hansom cab to the Beacon Hill Academy for Young Women where they were met, at the back door, by the headmistress, Miss Alma Veasley.

At first her mother came every Saturday—though she never got out of the waiting cab—to take Marnette out to dinner at some elegant and expensive restaurant, always in a different part of town. Then after a while, she came only every other Saturday.

When Marnette was in her second year at the boarding school, it was only once a month that her mother came, and toward the end, her visits had dwindled down to twice a year.

But long before then, Marnette had learned to be grateful for those long gaps between her mother's visits, for it was getting harder to look into the cold, dead-looking eyes of the woman who once had been so sweet and loving a mother. Even more painful were the other girls' whispers behind Marnette's back after her mother brought her back to the school.

At thirteen, Marnette still had not fully understood. Not until after one of those dinners out with her mother, when the headmistress had snidely asked her, "And where did the madam take you this time?"

In her almost four years at this finest of finishing schools, Marnette had often been told what a "lady" was, but she had no idea what a "madam" was. And in the hope of learning that, she had gone to the kitchen to ask the only friend she ever had: Katie Sullivan, the school's plump and red-faced Irish cook, at that moment up to her elbows in pastry dough.

"Madam?" said Katie, pausing in her kneading to give it a moment's thought. "Well, you might say that's when one tart gets the biggest slice of the pie."

Looking back on it later, Marnette was sure Katie Sullivan had no idea Marnette was asking about her own mother, else she surely would not have so glibly described Cynthia Coulter's unholy occupation.

Marnette had not seen her mother in more than six months, when she had come down one morning to find the newspaper beside her breakfast plate—and Alma Veasley, seated at the head of the long table, watching her face as she read.

Though the Boston police called it arson—some outraged citizen had finally set fire to a certain house of ill repute—the editor of the paper called it the wrath of God. Marnette still feared the editor had been right and that Cynthia Coulter was burning in hell.

Didn't the Good Book say something about the sins of a father being visited upon his son? Wouldn't the same be true of a mother and daughter? Especially a child conceived in sin?

There had been anything but a "Praise-the-Lord" look on Marnette's face when she had first climbed the steps of the Chappie Creek church three years ago, fearing God might strike her dead for daring to enter His holy house or that the pastor might see the scarlet letter on her own breast: a *B* that did not stand for Boston.

⁊

As she settled herself between her grandmother and cousin Emilie in the church pew this hot Sunday morning in June, Marnette felt the burden of another letter slowly being etched on her heart: an *L* for all the lies she had told her prairie family—as well as the lies she had told, two days ago, to someone in the woods.

But, if Ina Coulter had any idea that someone in the family was a liar, she never gave any sign. And on any Sunday morning, she was concerned with only one thing: that her family "kept holy the Sabbath Day." And she always insisted on getting to the church at least ten minutes before the morning worship service, "So we can all get into the proper mind for praising the Lord."

The family could have taken any one of the student-bench pews up front, but Ina always led them into the very last. Marnette was sure that was so her grandmother could see which of the "lost sheep" she had been praying for might have returned to the fold.

Marnette would not have been surprised if there were even more wayward sheep on such a steamy Sunday morning. Already sweltering herself in her starched bonnet and Sunday frock of white corded dimity, she now reached for one of the worn-out hymnals and began fanning herself.

She soon glanced sideways as their pastor came up the aisle to claim the teacher's platform that would serve as his pulpit until the town someday had a real church. Pastor Humphries also arrived early so he would be up on the platform to welcome his congregation as they came in: perspiring men, women, and children slowly shuffling in out of the hot June sun.

Although their widowed shepherd smiled and nodded as each family took its pew, to Marnette it was a heartsick little smile. And she, more than anyone else in the church, did not have to ask herself why.

Several months after she had settled in with her new family, Marnette had received an invitation from Sarah Humphries to come to the parsonage—really just another log cabin—for tea. After that it had become routine: two o'clock tea every Thursday with the pastor's pretty young wife.

At first, Marnette had dreaded those tea-sipping visits, because all Sarah wanted to talk about was back East, a world Marnette was trying so hard to forget. But before too long, she discovered what the pastor's wife so carefully hid from everyone else, perhaps even her husband: her undying homesickness for Hartford, Connecticut, and her aching loneliness when her husband rode the circuit every other month, ministering to his scattered flock in other prairie towns where there was neither a church nor a parson.

"But I'm sure *you'll* never be lonely," Sarah had told her on one of their early visits. "Indeed, you've caused quite a stir among the young men."

Marnette had merely lowered her eyes over her white china teacup. She was not ready to share with anyone—certainly not the pastor's prim and proper young wife—her thoughts about men.

Marnette could count on one hand the few men in Chappie Creek, besides Doc Britton, that she had come to trust. One, of course, was her Uncle Thad. And, though Stuart Whittington had not yet returned as he had promised, she still counted him among the trustworthy. Last, but not least, was Sarah Humphries' white-collared husband—even though Marnette did not believe in the loving and merciful God he so fervently preached about.

"In fact," said Sarah, refilling both of their cups, "I know of one young man who hasn't taken his eyes off you since the day you arrived. At least not in church."

Again Marnette was silent. She was only too aware of Drew Britton's glances from across the aisle.

"Paul looked at me the same way before he got the courage to come calling," said Sarah.

Marnette looked up in surprise. She could not believe the wife of any man of God would consider Drew Britton a satisfactory suitor for any young woman. Perhaps Sarah, so seldom leaving the parsonage, had never heard that awful song about him or learned about that terrible day in the woods.

Then another thought invaded Marnette's mind: Paul? She thought the pastor's first name was Richard.

"We were to be married," Sarah explained, "but Paul was struck down with diphtheria two weeks before the wedding. That's how it all began with Richard and me—I mean the Reverend. He was our pastor at the Hartford church, and he began coming to the house in the hope of comforting me."

Her pale blue eyes misted before she lowered them over her teacup. "If it weren't for him, I don't know how I could have lived through it. And that shows you how merciful the good Lord is."

Again Marnette stared at Sarah Humphries in disbelief. That was an act of mercy, striking down her young lover with a deadly disease and replacing him with a man almost old enough to be her father? And what soon happened to Sarah herself—was that the hand of a loving and merciful God?

Even on her very first visit, Marnette had thought the pastor's young wife was too thin and she had not been fooled by that artful brush of rouge on her so prominent cheekbones or her attempts at covering the little cough that came between every sentence or every other sip of tea.

"Just a nervous habit," Sarah feebly smiled when Marnette suggested a visit to Doc Britton.

But that winter it had become a much bigger cough, and before spring, Sarah Humphries' name had been carved into a gravestone on Massacre Hill.

That cold and lifeless stone—and the pearl-handled mirror and hairbrush that Sarah had given her just a week before she died—were Marnette's only mementos of the homesick young woman from Connecticut who, Marnette often sadly thought, might have become the second true friend in her life.

eight

Her eyes still on the Chappie Creek pastor, welcoming his sweaty Sunday morning congregation, Marnette again wondered if Sarah Humphries had ever come to love him. There was no doubt in anyone's mind, though, that the reverend had loved her.

In the year after Sarah had died, the older women—whispering at the bottom of the church steps—said it was only his deep faith in the Lord that kept their widowed pastor from despair.

But there were some who felt faith was not enough, especially when their pastor's mourning had gone into its second year. They had begun offering him a more tangible and earthly comfort: pushing their unmarried daughters closer and closer to the pulpit. Though he surely was over forty, there were many matchmaking mothers who thought the Reverend Richard Humphries would be a fine catch for any Chappie Creek girl.

Indeed, some older women, widows themselves, were suspected of attending weekly Bible study at the parsonage merely to be in their pastor's view should he finally end his long mourning and begin looking among his congregation for another wife.

And here comes one of them, Marnette thought as Leah Jaster walked up the aisle with her four children. It was no secret that the Widow Jaster was looking for another husband, but Marnette doubted even their pious pastor had faith (or fortitude) enough to put up with Leah's sharp tongue or her unruly, fatherless brood.

When her husband had died two winters ago, Leah had taken the boys out of school to help her with the family farm—a fact which Marnette, as temporary schoolmarm, had not lamented. Even Stuart Whittington, the stoutest of disciplinarians, had admitted the "two Jaster louts" had been more than he could handle.

Next to file into the stuffy church were the seven Newhouses, taking up two entire pews. Still fanning herself with one of the hymnals, Marnette watched as Grandma Newhouse began doing the same—probably the only use the little widowed matriarch had for any book, what with her eyesight being so poor. It was a blessing that she knew all the Sunday hymns by heart.

Though her son, Zachary, still had to use a hymnal, his voice was always one of the loudest whenever the congregation sang. At the "Praise-God-for-His-Blessings" part of last Sunday's service, Zachary Newhouse had loudly and clearly thanked the Lord for not letting the family perish in that fire the past week, omitting the fact that he himself—having spent the day sampling his latest batch of applejack—had started the fire by falling asleep in the loft with his corncob pipe.

Angus, Mattie, and Tim Piper were next in the procession of Sunday worshipers. Was Marnette imagining it, or was the elder Piper holding his head somewhat higher, now that his so sharp-minded son had been appointed town clerk?

Next were Douglas and Lorna Howlett with their three crisply starched and bonneted little girls, and yet another baby rumored to be on the way. Lorna Chappie had been only sixteen when she'd married Douglas Howlett, something unheard of in Boston. There, if your family had the means, you went to a finishing school until you were at least sixteen. Then there would be a coming out party, followed by at least two years of similar fetes where a girl could meet suitable young men, giving her—and more especially her parents—plenty of time to pick and choose.

When she did select a young man, there would be at least a year of closely chaperoned courtship. In Chappie Creek, you hardly knew a man and a girl had spoken to each other, and they were getting married.

Now it was Abbie Britton who came up the aisle, her usual plain self in pale yellow dimity. Or was it merely her strikingly beautiful, half-Indian sister, walking behind her in muted mauve, who made Drew Britton's twin sister seem so plain and colorless?

Marnette never saw either of the sisters that she did not regret turning down Abbie's continued invitations to her monthly sewing bees. But how was she to calmly sit and sew on even the simplest sampler with their brother under the same roof?

Marnette was especially sorry about never having befriended Abbie's sister. It was not only the young unmarried men who shied away from Wilting Sunflower. Their sisters, too, made sure they were never seen in public with this other young woman who had an indelible mark on her soul.

Directly behind the two Britton sisters came their father, looking as handsome as ever in his dark Sunday suit. Sitting beside Emilie, Marnette did not miss her cousin's lingering glance.

Was she right about Emilie's feelings for Doc Britton? If so, couldn't she—shouldn't she—spare her cousin a heap of heartbreak by telling her what she knew?

Maybe Emilie already knew and was hoping to change the doctor's mind about never marrying again. But even if he should lose his fear of burying another young wife, how could he take another woman into his home when he already had two potential old maids to provide for?

Last in the little parade of Brittons was the doctor's tall son in a starched white collar and gray broadcloth suit, causing many young female heads to turn in his direction—Marnette's included.

Though her Uncle Thad sat in reverent silence between his two sons at the other end of the pew, in her mind Marnette clearly heard what he had said at breakfast Friday about Drew Britton's secret courtship: *Everyone will know who when Drew takes her home from the Founders' Day ball.*

Had she been wrong about Drew's motive in waiting for her behind the schoolhouse the day before? Hadn't she thought, even then, that his invitation to go to the Founders' ball was somewhat vague?

While any Chappie Creek man might, indeed, be secretly courting some young woman in town, it certainly wouldn't be a secret to the girl herself!

The more she thought of their conversation that day in the woods, the more Marnette was convinced that Drew Britton had never asked her to the Founders Day ball.

Watching him take his seat beside his father, Marnette dared not ask herself what she was feeling fearing the answer might be disappointment.

❧

It was with something other than disappointment that Marnette sat waiting in the family buckboard—one of the few times she had not joined in the fellowship outside the church after the Sunday service was over. After the pastor's hour-long sermon, and before he had dismissed his sweltering congregation, Pastor Humphries had made two announcements, as requested by the Chappie Creek Town Council. The first was the appointment of Tim Piper as town clerk and Drew Britton as town constable, news that sent a murmur of approval throughout the steamy church.

It was the second announcement that brought groans from at least twelve children in church that morning: They were to come back to the schoolhouse a week from Monday to begin rehearsing the Founders' Day children's pageant their temporary schoolmarm had "so graciously volunteered" to direct.

It wouldn't have been so bad for Marnette, if the pastor hadn't added, "Since no one has yet had any word from Stuart

Whittington," informing one member of the congregation that she had told some whopping lies that day in the woods.

Finally the churchyard visiting ended and the rest of the family climbed into the buckboard for the ride home, her uncle taking the reins after helping Marnette's grandmother onto the seat beside him.

"Why do I get the feeling, Ma," he asked her, "that the reverend was scolding us?"

"Because he was," said Ina Coulter.

Sorely aware of Drew Britton's smug I-knew-she-was-lying expression across the aisle, Marnette had not been looking for any hidden meaning in their pastor's parting words: "Let us not, in all our patriotic fervor, forget the true Founder, the Creator of this great and glorious land. Let us never fail to seek first the kingdom of God."

"He was only saying what I've told you all along," said her grandmother with a scornful nod toward the town's new brick meeting hall. "We should have built a decent church first."

Her son looked at the almost-finished building before flicking the reins. "Well, we can blame Stu Whittington for that."

"Foogh!" huffed his mother. "He only put the idea into your heads. It was you seven sheep on the town council who voted for it."

She was not the only one in Chappie Creek who had spoken against building a town hall—especially the expense of buying and shipping those wagonloads of red bricks. Some of the settlers had balked, too, at the idea of forming a town council until their schoolmaster—living one month with one family and the next with another—had finally convinced the stubborn prairie folk that they needed some form of local government.

"Some crazy idea he got out of a book," was the way Angus Piper had put it. Angus thought book learning was a waste of time, despite the fact that it was at the schoolhouse that his son, Tim, had learned to keep such accurate accounts for him.

Maybe having their own local government *was* something Stuart Whittington had gotten out of a book, but it was also something that worked back East and in other small towns that had sprung up as people had begun moving westward from New England.

When the schoolmaster got on his pet subject, always at mealtime, it seemed he would eat twice as much. And Marnette would wonder if her grandmother was glad he was not living with them permanently and next month would bed-and-boarded with another Chappie Creek family.

"How can they be so pigheaded—so stupid?" he would ask Marnette's uncle, reaching for another helping of meat. "They boast about George Washington, Tom Jefferson, and Paul Revere, and then forget the very thing it was all about—independence! Here they have it in the palms of their hands, the chance for self government, and they can't even see it!"

Maybe that was because so many of the townsfolk thought *government* meant *punishment.* What did Chappie Creek need a town council for, when there were so many woodsheds handy? The only serious crime ever committed in town had been the massacre over twenty years ago, and the real culprit had already gone to his just reward. And as for Drew Britton's sending him there, Marnette Coulter had yet to find anyone else in town who called that a crime.

It was not until that last wagon train had arrived and six more cabins had sprung up along the creek, that the people began to understand what their schoolmaster was talking about.

Who decided where a fence should begin and where it should end? Who should decide whether a new road should run east-west or north-south? And just how many menfolk were to stop their own work to build that road? If they should be paid for such back-breaking work, where was the money to come from?

The answer was taxes. And in order for each family to pay its fair share, someone had to levy and collect those taxes, as well as make the rules about boundaries and roads: a body of respected and reasonably intelligent men chosen by the townsfolk (that is, the men) themselves.

The first town meeting had been held two years ago at the schoolhouse, with Stuart Whittington presiding. Before the evening was over, the town had its first board of seven councilmen: Claymore Britton, Thaddeus Coulter, Angus Piper, Chester York, Zachary Newhouse, Douglas Howlett, and Bryce Doolittle.

A month later—at the continued urging of the schoolmaster—the town council had unanimously voted to build a town hall. Their next vote was to officially dedicate that hall on August 1, 1848, the day on which, fifty years before, the first settlers had arrived. It would be called Founders' Day in honor of Leo and Lorna Chappie—now both dead—who had built the first crude cabin along the creek.

Now Marnette Coulter—the newest settler in town and the one who probably knew the least about it—was to create and direct a children's pageant portraying the history of Chappie Creek.

જ

Up front in the family wagon, Ina Coulter was engaged in her own bit of oral history: who had, or had not, come to church that Sunday morning. "I'm still not sure we even need one," she said, "but I'd wager we have ourselves the handsomest town constable on the whole prairie." She glanced back at Marnette and Emilie. "Wouldn't you girls agree?"

Marnette said nothing, inwardly red-faced at having unwittingly been exposed by their pastor as a liar. She also had the feeling her grandmother was fishing for clues, as to whether she might have missed something going on right under her nose: one of her look-alike granddaughters having a secret romance with their new town constable.

Emilie put her straight about one of them. "If I ever set my cap for any Britton, Grandma, it wouldn't be Drew."

Ina Coulter merely chuckled. It was no secret that most women in town—young or old—thought the town's handsome widowed doctor might also be a fine catch.

Still, Marnette was surprised that her mind-reading grandmother could not see what was so obvious: Emilie's attraction to Doctor Claymore Britton.

"You'd have yourself a battle with Leah Jaster," said Emilie's father, turning the wagon onto the rutted roadway leading to his farm. "I hear tell that after all those sick calls at the widow's cabin, the doc finally found the cure. Taking her to the Founders' Day ball."

nine

Poor Emilie, Marnette thought on her way to the schoolhouse a week later—a week in which she had finished two of the other ladies' ball gowns, keenly aware that her cousin had not taken a single stitch more on the gown she was making for herself. She was sure that meant Emilie, to spare herself an evening of heartache, no longer planned on going to the Founders' Day ball.

She herself had never intended to go to the August ball, but having been shanghaied into directing the children's pageant, there was no way, short of breaking a leg, that she could absent herself from the evening's festivities. Besides, now that she knew Drew Britton was secretly courting someone else, there was no reason for her to stay at home—or to take the long way to the schoolhouse, for that matter.

Nevertheless, she was glad to find that, with all the bricklaying finished, the town hall builders were working inside.

Even though she had taken the shorter route—still a long walk from home—some of the children were waiting for her on the schoolhouse steps. All five of them were girls, three of them brand new faces: girls whose parents had been reluctant to let them waste their time going to school, but who had no aversion to seeing their little darlings up on a stage—even if it meant some undone, or at least postponed, chores back home during the weeks of rehearsals before Founders' Day.

If Marnette had not come to the schoolhouse this Monday morning, she herself might be scrubbing her knuckles bare, helping Emilie with the first of the week's washings. *Hardly a fitting task for any china doll*, she wryly thought, never quite able to forget Drew's brash assessment of her the day she had arrived in Chappie Creek.

Her grandmother, too, had at first treated her like some fragile piece of porcelain in need of careful handling. But after those first few weeks of coddling, Ina Coulter had apparently decided that the most loving thing she could do for her long-lost granddaughter was to prepare her for the hardships she would eventually face as some man's wife in this or some other crude town out on the prairie.

Marnette had suddenly found herself with a share of the chores at her uncle's cabin: scrubbing floors, washing and mending clothes, cleaning, baking, stuffing sausages and curing meat, picking and drying berries, making soap, cooking meals, and churning butter. Ina Coulter deemed that these and several other tedious and time-consuming tasks were necessary to maintain a peaceful and orderly household for the farmer son who had so blessedly taken her under his roof.

With her temporary job as schoolmarm, Marnette had escaped most of those chores for the past six months. Though she would be free of them for at least another six weeks, this morning she knew she had no easy task awaiting her in the stuffy schoolhouse: trying to make actors out of children who themselves had never seen any kind of stage play. And grabbing the attention of the ten rough-and-tumble boys who thought they had seen the last of the schoolhouse until September would be no easy task, either.

Maybe none of those boys would show up, Marnette thought as she went into the schoolhouse and began opening windows. They were even more sorely needed by their families during the field-hoeing, wood-chopping, pig-fattening summer. And even if they were excused from such necessary chores, most of them would probably fear that being up on a stage would brand them as sissies.

By the time she had all the windows open and three more

girls had arrived, Marnette was convinced her pantomimed history of Chappie Creek would have an all-girl cast.

But before too long, the boys began straggling in. By nine o'clock all ten of them were there, and Marnette had eighteen players—ten boys and eight girls—for the town's very first stage play.

She didn't understand the boys' reaction—some of them made outright castor oil faces—when she told them about her planned pantomime production until she recalled that their pastor, in announcing the event from his pulpit a week ago, had merely called it "a children's show." No doubt each of the boys had his own idea about the kind of show it should be.

"A circus," Davy Doolittle told her, the first to raise his hand when Marnette began polling them. This was not too surprising from a boy who spent most of the school lunch hour doing cartwheels and handstands to amuse the girls.

"A magic show," said young Chester York, next to raise his hand. Chestie was an expert at making himself invisible whenever there was either water or wood to be brought into the schoolhouse.

"Or a pet show," was Willie Christopher's hope. Willie rarely came to school without some little wild woodland creature trying to get out of his pocket.

"Those are all excellent ideas," Marnette assured the three boys, "but the town council thought the pageant should have something to do with Chappie Creek and how it got started."

All ten boys again made squarish mouths.

"I'm sure Ma and Pa Chappie didn't find it so dull," Marnette insisted. "Not with all those wild animals—and all those Indians lurking behind the trees."

She remembered her own fear, three years ago, at the band of Indians watching at the side of the road. But that was before she had grown so accustomed to all those animal-trapping Indians coming into the trading post with their furs. And before she had learned that she herself was part Indian.

"You mean we can show the Indians and stuff like that?" asked Davy Doolittle, brightening somewhat.

"Everything any of you can remember," Marnette nodded. "Anything your parents or grandparents may have told you about the past."

Marnette was sure that was how a town without any writers—or many readers—passed its history on: in bedtime stories around the fire and the old-timers' stories told at meeting places like the trading post. In Chappie Creek, though, she suspected some of those latter tales had some embellishment, as one crusty old storyteller tried to outdo another.

But even back in Boston, Marnette had known that a lot of New England families had gone by wagon train much farther west than Chappie Creek, most of them to pick up the Oregon Trail which had been trampled out, first by the Indians and trappers, and then by adventuresome men like Lewis and Clark.

Though many men had gone alone, entire families had also taken the long and dangerous journey—and not a few of those families had left a trail of shallow graves behind.

The ever-beckoning lure to go west was gold. And though Leo Chappie may also have started out in the hope of striking it rich, he and his young wife Lorna had found a different gold —open and fertile flatlands that they were sure would yield rich harvests. They had never gone farther than the small winding creek that would later bear their name, building the first small cabin that now stood empty on the outskirts of town. One of many cabins that had given Marnette serious doubts about living in Chappie Creek when she had first arrived.

"We'll start," she now told her young pageant players, "by choosing a boy and a girl to be Pa and Ma Chappie."

Though this caused a little stir of excitement among the girls, the boys were again something less than enthusiastic.

It was too bad, Marnette thought, that Lorna Howlett's

oldest girl was still so young. As the great granddaughter of Leo and Lorna Chappie, she would have been the perfect one to play the part of Ma Chappie.

As it was, Marnette ended up granting the roles of the first Chappie Creek couple to Dale Newhouse and Nancy Mae Cunningham. Which caused another twitter among the other girls, because they all knew Dale was sweet on Nancy Mae.

Following the wagon ride west, next in the pantomimed history of Chappie Creek would be the memorable day on which Leo Chappie had made peace with the chief of the neighboring Indian tribe. Marnette gave the role of Chief Howling Wolf to Jeremy Sands because he was the only boy who could fold his arms and look stony, like a real Indian chief, without laughing.

Despite the ever-mounting heat in the schoolroom, the pageant players and their director slowly moved forward in chronicling their town's history, eventually arriving at two important happenings which Marnette wished they had all forgotten.

There was no shortage of volunteers among the remaining eight boys to play the band of brandy-sodden Indians who had swooped down on the town from Massacre Hill that infamous summer day.

"No," Marnette said quietly, "I don't think we should include that."

"Why not?" demanded Davy Doolittle. "Everybody knows it happened."

"That's true," Marnette nodded. *And there still are some who would like to forget it,* she added to herself. "But let's just skip over that for now. I'll think about it at home, later, and decide just how we might handle that."

She let out a little sigh of relief at the boys' reluctant acceptance of her postponement. Relief that quickly died when one of the other boys brought up the town's other tragic happening in the woods. Every one of the boys knew exactly how to portray it, and they almost came to blows, fighting for the two male roles.

Davy Doolittle finally settled the squabble over one of those roles. The tallest boy in the room—and also the only one with light enough hair—Davy stood up and stoutly announced: "I'll be him!"

Marnette did not have to ask who Davy was going to be, even if he had not so aptly fit the part. For he made it perfectly clear by raising and aiming an imaginary rifle.

And then there was a sea of waving hands and shouts of "Me! Me!" from every other boy—begging for the part of Otis Grimes.

"You!" said Davy, turning and aiming his phantom flintlock at Willie Christopher in the rear of the room. "Ka-pow!"

Crossing his eyes, Willie threw his hands up to his head and slowly slid off his seat and onto the floor. A sudden burst of applause filled the stuffy room.

Then someone began singing it and before long, all eighteen children were singing:

> *'Twas in the woods*
> *at early morn,*
> *A brand new day*
> *just barely born;*
>
> *Most Chappie Creek*
> *folks still abed,*
> *Young Drew shot. . .*

"Stop it!" Marnette screamed. "Stop it this very second!"

Because no one had ever kept them from singing the song before, the students fell silent, looking at their schoolmarm with round, wondering eyes.

"I think you should all go home now," she told them in a

quieter, though still shaky, voice. "We'll start off fresh tomorrow morning."

❧

That night, as she lay in the dark beside Emilie in the big canopied bed, the children's unfinished song kept ringing in Marnette's head. And there was no way she could stop it from reaching its end: *Young Drew shot Crazy Otis dead.*

Nor could she dispel the vision of the other wounded player in that bloody drama in the woods: Wilting Sunflower, with a look of stark naked terror on her face.

It was with that haunting vision that Marnette finally fell into a fitful sleep, only to wake, in the middle of the night, to her own nightmarish scream.

ten

Marnette knew one more stagecoach was due in Chappie Creek before Founders' Day, and she still hoped the long-absent (and silent) schoolmaster would be on it. There had not, of course, been even the smallest of notes with the latest book he had sent her: a small volume of verse by someone with the curious name of Percy Bysshe Shelley.

Nor had she had the time to open the book again—spending her mornings at the schoolhouse rehearsing the children's pageant and her afternoons at her uncle's cabin, feverishly sewing on other ladies' ball gowns. She might not have felt so rushed if she hadn't taken that last order from Leah Jaster.

Ordinarily, the Chappie Creek women made or mended their own everyday dresses of sturdy calico or muslin. Only when they wanted a fancier Sunday or calling dress of poplin or chintz did they bring the pattern and material to the town's most skilled—and lately most speedy—seamstress.

But Leah Jaster had come to the cabin—luckily, the night that Emilie was at the parsonage for Bible study—with neither fabric nor form. She had merely thumbed through Marnette's dog-eared copy of Godey's Lady's Book, found the fanciest and fullest gown, and told Marnette: "There! Just like that!" She also told Marnette that her Founders' Day ball gown must be fashioned of nothing less than the finest on Farnsworth's shelf.

This meant, of course, that Marnette had to make a special Saturday trip to the trading post. And because Ina Coulter had discovered she was out of a number of store-bought staples, Emilie—armed with a long written list—accompanied her to the post. Indeed, Emilie drove the buckboard: another unheard of doing in Boston.

Marnette wished that she herself had learned to drive the wagon and could have gone to the trading post by herself that morning. How was she to choose the fabric for Leah Jaster's ball gown without Emilie wondering who it was for?

She decided that, if Emilie should ask, she would tell her this latest gown was for herself, adding another to her growing list of lies. But wasn't her whole life in Chappie Creek founded on lies?

On Saturday, the Chappie Creek town square was always alive with activity, many of the townsfolk coming into the trading post for store-bought sugar, salt, and spices shipped from New England. The neighboring Indians also drifted in: the men with their animal skins and the women to trade baskets or blankets for the little glass beads with which they decorated their dresses and moccasins and the buckskin tunics of their men.

Though everyone knew this was not the same tribe involved in the massacre—that tribe had simply vanished in the night—they were Indians, nonetheless, and were thereby guilty. Every now and then one of the Indian fur-traders would end up with a broken nose or collar bone after a mysterious (but never witnessed) fall down the trading post steps. Farnsworth himself boasted of his personal in-store revenge by sometimes adding a few stones when he weighed out the women's glass beads.

Though Marnette's grandmother rarely went to the trading post, she was aware of the danger, there, to any full-blooded Indian. And only a few nights ago, at supper, she had lamented the latest incident of an Indian fur-trader "falling" down the steps and landing face-down in the dirt.

"And we call ourselves Christians," she had said, shaking her graying head, as if the whole town, herself included, shared the guilt of a few.

Marnette supposed it was hard for her grandmother, half white and half Indian, to be constantly torn between two allegiances. But Ina Coulter was first and foremost a Christian, and there could be no fence-sitting when it came to the teaching of Jesus about loving one's enemies. Besides, these were not even the same Indians who had committed the massacre for which some people in town still sought revenge.

"I'm sure those trading post steps will be safer," said her son, Thaddeus, "now that we have a town constable to keep an eye on things there."

Knowing Doc Britton often rode out to the Indian village to bring medicine to the sick, he was sure the doctor's son would not allow any more "accidents" back in town.

But Ina Coulter had her own thoughts about the need for an officer of the law. And if her son thought she would accept this latest argument in its favor, he was wrong.

"Well, to do that—he'd have to be sitting on those steps, night and day."

As Emilie and Marnette approached the trading post, that Saturday morning, Marnette saw that Drew was in fact sitting on the trading post steps, whittling on a piece of wood.

With the empty stagecoach also at the hitching post, Marnette had no trouble interpreting the smug look on Drew's face: a look which plainly told her that Stuart Whittington had not been among the coach's incoming passengers. The town's new law officer knew, for certain, that Marnette had given him false testimony about the missing schoolmaster that day in the woods.

But, surrounded by his usual audience of spellbound children, the town's favorite woodcarver merely nodded at Emilie's "hello" as the two cousins passed him on the stairs. Marnette, her sunbonneted head turned aside, pretended not to have seen him.

Once inside, she snapped to Emilie, "I didn't know being the town's peace officer meant entertaining its children." She was really cross with herself for his having caught her in a lie.

"Everyone knows carving is Drew's real love," said Emilie. "And if he lived in some big city, like Boston, he might even make a living with it."

Marnette wondered if her cousin wasn't right. Though she had never seen any of the little figures Drew Britton carved for the children, she had often admired some wooden figurines in the window of one of the city's gift shops a block away from the Beacon Hill Academy.

Marnette gave herself a mental shake. How the doctor's son might make a living was no concern of hers, especially when the whole town would soon find out who he would be supporting for the rest of his life.

"Besides," said Emilie, "he's probably here today, just to keep an eye on his sister." She glanced around, as if sure she would find one of Drew's sisters in some corner of the post.

Marnette knew which sister her cousin meant. She had been in Chappie Creek only a few months when she had learned that wherever Wilting Sunflower might go, her half brother was sure to be close behind. She had wondered about his constant shadowing until she had heard the story about him and Otis Grimes. The storytellers never said it in so many words, but they strongly hinted that while there wasn't a man in town who would take Wilting Sunflower for his wife, there were some men who might not hesitate to have their way with her.

After that, Marnette herself had kept a pitying eye on the comings and goings of Drew Britton's half sister, and today was one of the few times she had come to the trading post that Wilting Sunflower was not also browsing in the Ladies' Department. It seemed that on each of those occasions, Tim Piper had also been "browsing" in another corner.

No. Marnette refused to believe something like that about Tim Piper. Or Wilting Sunflower, for that matter.

"Well," she sighed to Emilie with a nod toward the ladies'

corner, "I've got to look for some decent fabric for another ball gown."

"How about burlap?" suggested Emilie.

It was a harmless little quip, but it stopped Marnette in her tracks. What was Emilie telling her—that she knew who had ordered this latest of gowns? But, of course! Anyone in the family might have mentioned Leah Jaster's gown-ordering visit the night Emilie had gone to Bible study.

Well, there was one way to find out. "So Doc Britton's taking Leah to the ball," she admitted. "That doesn't mean he's going to marry her."

Emilie said nothing. But her face said everything: that Marnette had been right about her feelings for the town's doctor. And that Emilie was sure Marnette's next order would be for the Widow Jaster's wedding gown.

At that moment Homer Farnsworth came shuffling over to hand Marnette a small brown packet. "This'll save the boy from having to run over with it," was all he said, going back to his counter before she could thank him.

The face of the packet—actually a large envelope—was addressed to "Miss Marie Antoinette Coulter." Recognizing the schoolmaster's flowery script, Marnette knew it was, finally, a letter from Stuart Whittington!

"I'd better begin on Grandma's list," said Emilie, sounding relieved at not having to respond to Marnette's comment about Leah Jaster and Doc Britton.

Having waited so long for a letter from the schoolmaster, Marnette wasted no time in opening it once she was alone in the ladies' corner. She had barely read the beginning when she leaned against the fabric table for support—almost floored by the letter's contents.

> *My Dear Marie Antoinette,*
>   *Please forgive my long silence, but so much*

has happened since I arrived in Boston, I simply did not have the time, until now, to sit down and write a coherent letter to either you or the school board, explaining why I will not be returning to Chappie Creek.

Not returning!

Something totally unforeseen (but certainly not unfortunate) happened during the settlement of my late uncle's estate: my meeting a distant cousin who had sadly been widowed two years ago. Quite frankly, I instantly fell madly in love with this most beautiful lady.

Madly in love? Old Muttonchops?

To make a long and perhaps unbelievable story short, my dear, not long after settling the estate, Norma and I returned to the courthouse to attend to another matter: obtaining a license for our marriage and setting the wheels in motion for my legally adopting her three fatherless little girls.

Married? Three children?

But even that—our being married in church two months ago—is not the happiest part of my story, my dear. The most blessed thing is that, even before we were joined in holy wedlock, Norma had—by her true and abiding faith—led me to also accept Jesus as my Lord and Savior.

I can hear your grandmother now, praising

the Lord at learning that the town's heathen schoolmaster has finally seen the light. You can assure her that every day I, too, praise our merciful Lord for not only blessing me with such a beautiful wife and ready-made family, but giving me salvation, as well.

But enough about me. What I am concerned about now, my dear, is your future. (Not that I worry about your salvation, for I know how faithful you are in worshiping the Lord every Sunday.) I am talking about the here and now.

I am sure you have been performing just splendidly at the schoolhouse in my long absence. I have written the school board (letter enclosed) not only tendering my formal resignation as the Chappie Creek schoolmaster, but also recommending you as my permanent replacement—if that is what you wish. But I urge you, my dear, to seriously consider another option: that of your returning to Boston, to live with me and my new family. I have already discussed this with Mrs. Whittington and she is wholeheartedly in favor of (indeed, excited about) the idea.

If you are wondering whether we would have enough room, wonder no more. For we have moved into the home I inherited from my uncle— a spacious mansion with no less than five bedrooms—and one of those rooms has already been reserved for you.

Before you are even tempted to protest that you would be a financial burden on this family of five, let me assure you, my dear, that not only did I inherit the big house, but a modest bank account as well. Besides, I intend to soon seek a

*new teaching position here in Boston—for I am
sure you know that, even if I were a millionaire, I
could not bear to remain idle—and with that
additional income, I can easily afford a sixth
member of this family.*

    *But if you should be adamant about "earning
your keep" with the Boston Whittingtons, I have
an answer for that, too: your serving as governess to our three little girls. This not only would
be most advantageous to Norma—freeing her to
devote even more time to her works of charity—
it would, I believe, also be advantageous to you.
For, living in Boston, you would have the
opportunity to meet young men of good character and genteel manners. And that, my dear, is
what I have always feared: that one of those
Chappie Creek barbarians might someday
persuade you to marry him.*

    *That is not at all the life I wish for you, my
dear, becoming just another work-worn drudge
in some drafty cabin out on the prairie. That
may be all some other girls can hope for, but for
a young lady of your delicate frame and excellent upbringing...*

For a second time Marnette almost choked, the first being at
his reference to her faithful Sunday worshiping.

She only briefly scanned the rest of his letter: all about what
she need, and need not, bring with her if and when she returned to Boston. She had just refolded the letter when she
looked up to see the Chappie Creek town constable striding
toward her, and she quickly stuffed it and the envelope into
her drawstringed reticule. But not quite fast enough.

"Only a letter?" he said somewhat dryly. Again a seemingly

harmless little quip, except that Marnette knew what he really meant: that, if Stuart Whittington was to be back in time to take her to the Founders' Day ball, he would have had to be on that mail-carrying stagecoach this morning.

Was that why the town constable had been out on the trading post steps—waiting for the monthly stage? Waiting for proof of the schoolmarm's lie? But why? Why should it be so important for a man who was courting one girl to let another know he had caught her in a lie?

"Yes," she told him, "a letter from Mister Whittington, apologizing for the delay." Though she had somewhat tardily opted for honesty, she omitted the fact that Stuart Whittington was not coming back at all.

"Which means," he said, just as dryly, "that a certain young lady will be coming alone to the Founders' Day ball."

Again it was like that day in the woods—his never mentioning her name. Nor did she give him any answer.

"Then I think," he said in an even drier tone yet, "that, as the town constable, it would be my duty to give that young lady prior warning. That any unescorted girl at the ball is considered fair game."

Again she didn't answer him, mostly because she wasn't sure what he meant. But also because it was just then that Emilie came to tell her the trader's grandson was loading up the buckboard for their trip back home.

❧

Before too long, the two cousins were on their way home with their grandmother's two crates of staples and the string-tied parcel of fabric for Leah Jaster's ball gown: twelve yards of flowered chintz and a skein of velvet ruching.

Emilie said nothing about either this latest gown or what it did or did not mean that Doc Britton was taking the widow to the Founders' Day ball. But she did ask Marnette about the letter that had come on the monthly stage. "From Mister

Whittington?"

"Yes," Marnette nodded. And she shared some of its surprising contents. "Can you believe that—that a middle-aged man would want to marry a widow with three small children?"

"Yes," Emilie nodded, "I can believe that." And Marnette knew she was not merely talking about the former schoolmaster.

Marnette sighed as she retied the strings of her sunbonnet, not knowing what she could do, or say, to change her cousin's mind about staying home from the ball. She was thinking, too, about her own attendance at that first-time event, only two weeks away.

"What does it mean, Emilie, for a girl to be fair game?"

"You mean at the ball?"

Marnette nodded.

"It means that any girl who comes without an escort," she flicked the reins, "is making herself available to any man without a partner."

"Available?"

"For dancing," said Emilie. "And being taken home by the one who claims the very last dance."

eleven

"I wish I had listened to Grandma," Marnette shivered, stepping out of her best dandelion dimity to let the yards of yellow corded cotton fall in a soggy heap on the bedroom floor.

"You weren't the only one who didn't believe it was going to rain," said Emilie, unbuttoning her own damp dress.

With so many weeks of cloudless skies, Marnette had not considered the possibility of rain when she had planned the end of the Founders' Day children's pageant: both players and audience walking from the new town hall up to Massacre Hill to hear Pastor Humphries deliver a very post-mortem eulogy honoring Ma and Pa Chappie and all the other early Chappie Creek settlers who lay beneath the sod.

"Besides, I didn't hear anyone complaining," said Emilie. "The Reverend himself said he thought it was most solemn and dignified."

Marnette gave her a little twisted smile. For they both knew the earlier part of the children's pageant had been anything but solemn or dignified.

The early events in the history of Chappie Creek had been portrayed by the children in pantomime—with Marnette narrating from the sidelines—up on the council platform at their new town hall. While some of it may have been more fiction than fact, the audience (mostly the parents of the eighteen players) politely sat through such historic happenings as:

. . .Leo and Lorna Chappie bouncing over the prairie in their covered wagon, discovering the creek, and then Leo chopping trees and building the very first log cabin of the settlement.

. . .The warning arrow being shot into the door of that cabin

89

and Leo Chappie angrily riding on horseback to take the arrow right back to its sender.

. . .Chief Howling Wolf trying to hide his amazement at the white man's bravery and the handshake and smoking of the peace pipe by the two neighbors.

The part the audience seemed to like best was when Chief Howling Wolf—so fittingly sober-faced during all those weeks of rehearsal—began snickering as Leo Chappie shook the arrow in his face.

Outside of that, as well as a few awkward pauses and some unrehearsed nose-scratchings and sneezes, the rest of the pantomimed history of Chappie Creek came out as planned: a moving chronicle of the town's growth. As it got closer to the present, murmurs of fond remembrance rose up from some of the older folks in the audience.

Marnette thought she heard some questioning murmurs, too, when the play came to an end with the present (the first town council meeting and the building of the town hall) without so much as having hinted at that bloody day on Massacre Hill.

And maybe that was why there had been no complaints when immediately after, to an ominous rumble of thunder, the entire assemblage had solemnly marched up to Massacre Hill to witness perhaps another historical event: a shortened-due-to-rain oration by their notoriously long-winded pastor, after which two of the men nailed a huge wreath of evergreens to one of the big oak trees that stood guard over all the Chappie Creek graves.

Though Marnette had not thought of it earlier, she was glad that Otis Grimes had been buried on the opposite, otherwise graveless side of the hill, and that even the end of the Founders' Day pageant would not evoke any memories of that unhappy day.

Only the Reverend Peter Pruett and three other menfolk had buried Otis Grimes on the opposite side of the hill—away from all those other townsfolk whose senseless slaughter he had caused. It had all been very quiet and very quick, as if everyone wanted to get it over and done with.

Was that the way it had been with her mother, Marnette suddenly wondered, standing in the rain on Massacre Hill: quick and quiet, to get it over and done with? Was there even a marker on her grave?

She knew there was someone in Chappie Creek who cared enough, or was simply Christian enough, to place violets on Otis Grimes' grave every spring. But who would ever visit the grave of Cynthia Coulter when her own daughter didn't know how—or where—she was buried?

Suddenly Marnette had trouble swallowing. Shivering, not only from the rain, she was relieved when the big pine wreath was finally nailed to the tree and she could turn her back on Massacre Hill. She would never come back, she promised herself, not even to visit Sarah Humphries' grave. Not when she knew the graveyard had the power to unearth thoughts she had been so sure were safely buried three years ago.

ஐ

"You're not going back, are you?" Emilie now asked, gathering both of their wet dresses up from the bedroom floor.

Her mind still on Boston, the question caught Marnette off guard. Had her cousin found Stuart Whittington's long letter and read the part she had never shared: his proposal that she come back to Boston to live with him and his new family? No, Emilie would never invade Marnette's so well-guarded privacy.

What her cousin was asking, Marnette realized, was whether or not she would be going back to the town hall for the box lunch social, the first of many scheduled post-pageant activities: hoop-rolling, pie-eating, and log-splitting contests in the adjacent schoolyard, as well as a three-legged race and a tug-of-war. And last, but not least, the Founders' Day ball that evening.

"No," Marnette told her. "I think the rest of Founders' Day can go on very well without me."

The sudden downpour had turned into a slow drizzle that had stopped even before they had gotten home. But it had been enough to send everyone on the hill home for a change of clothes: an inconvenience for most, but to Marnette a blessing in disguise. Not having had the time to think twice about making herself a new gown for the ball, she had planned on wearing the best of what she already had: the drenched yellow dimity now in her cousin's arms. And with the sky still over-cast—and their grandmother having claimed the hearth for baking—there was no way the dress could be dried and then pressed for wearing tonight: a perfect excuse for not going to the ball.

Indeed, Marnette had yet to attend any of the town's holiday dances, some of them held in her own uncle's barn. And while her sudden convenient headaches had come mainly to avoid Drew Britton—something she knew, now, she had not really needed to worry about—she still was not eager to be fair game tonight for any other young, unattached man at the Founders' Day ball.

"But you are going back tonight?" persisted Emilie.

"How can I?" Marnette nodded to the crumpled gown in her cousin's arms.

That stopped Emilie short. For, if she were to find holes in Marnette's excuse for not going to the ball—having nothing decent to wear—she would be destroying her own.

"But I thought you'd be taking my place at the refreshments table," she finally said. "And who's going to bring all those tarts?" she added with a nod toward the cabin's main room.

Their grandmother, having made her prediction of rain, had stayed home that morning not only to bake the week's supply of bread, but also to prepare the six dozen raspberry tarts that were to be the Coulter family's contribution to the sweets table that night.

And while she was only beginning on the tarts now, there was the matter of later bringing them to the town hall and arranging them on the table, along with the other women's pastries and the big punch bowl—Emilie's job as head of the Founders' Day refreshments committee.

"You have over six hours," said Marnette. "That's time enough to finish your gown." She knew all Emilie needed to do to finish her set-aside ball gown was sew on a small bit of trim and hem up the skirt.

Emilie opened her mouth as if to protest and then quickly closed it. Had she been about to admit her real reason for not going to the ball—to spare herself the heartache of watching Doc Britton dance the night away with Leah Jaster?

"You're absolutely right," Emilie said, totally surprising Marnette. "I have more than enough time."

Only later would Marnette understand her cousin's sudden change of heart and the determination with which she dumped both of their damp dresses into the hamper and went to their shared armoire for her not-quite-finished ball gown.

Standing in her damp petticoat, Marnette was trying to understand her own heart: her relief at having been spared a night of watching one of the Britton men dancing with someone else.

Having been assured by both Grandma and Emilie that neither of them needed her help, Marnette found herself with something she had not had in over six months: some free time. And she used some of that time in getting into her flannel robe and deciding what to do next: answer Stuart Whittington's letter or read the latest book he had sent her from Boston. Assuring herself that there was no urgency in answering the letter, she decided in favor of Percy Bysshe Shelley's little volume of verse. She took it from her nightstand drawer to lay down with it on the canopied bed.

Though she no longer wondered about the schoolmaster's capacity for romance, Marnette was still somewhat mystified by his choice of literature: that such a staunch after-the-fact supporter of the American Revolution would so consistently gift her with the works of writers who were all British.

She quickly scanned the table of contents of the new book until one of the poetic titles—"Love's Philosophy"—intrigued her enough to turn to that page and begin reading:

> *The fountains mingle with the river,*
> *And the rivers with the ocean,*
> *The winds of heaven mix forever*
> *With a sweet emotion;*
>
> *Nothing in the world is single;*
> *All things by a law divine*
> *In one spirit meet and mingle,*
> *Why not I with thine?*
>
> *See the mountains kiss high heaven*
> *And the waves clasp one another;*
> *No sister-flower would be forgiven*
> *If it disdained its brother;*
>
> *And the sunlight clasps the earth*
> *And the moonbeams kiss the sea;*
> *What is all this sweet work worth*
> *If thou kiss not me?*

Closing her eyes, Marnette wondered who the "thou" was for whom the poet Shelley had written such soulful words— what he must have been feeling for her to want to write them.

Was that what Stuart Whittington meant by falling madly in love? Had Doc Britton felt that way about either, or both, of his two young wives? Had her Uncle Thad felt that way about Emilie's mother? Might her own father have once felt that way about her mother?

"You never talk about your mother, Marnie," Emilie had said one night after they had gotten into the big canopied bed that had been Thad Coulter's wedding gift to his young bride.

Marnette had said nothing, totally unprepared for her cousin's personal comment after so many years.

"Was she pretty?"

"Yes," Marnette had finally answered. "She was pretty."

But Cynthia Coulter had been more than pretty, even with a swollen cheek and a blackened eye. How could it have ended like that, if her father had ever truly loved her mother? Was it all that whiskey that had killed his love? Or had there always been a demon inside of Thomas Coulter that the whiskey had slowly given control? Might not every man have such a demon?

Homer Farnsworth, for one. Was the trader really only a harmless old storyteller—or might his medicinal use of whiskey someday reveal a spirit anything but harmless?

Who but their own families knew what all the men in Chappie Creek were really like? Who, but the ones who lived with them, knew what went on behind the closed doors of all those log cabins?

Take Cyrus Gage who ran the lumber mill. Wasn't he already notorious as a skinflint, giving only the strictest measure in filling an order for wood? Might he not also demand of his wife, Adeline, an even stricter accounting of every scrap left over from a meal? Was that why Addie Gage would be another missing person at the ball tonight—because in his miserly thrift, her husband had not allowed her to make (or order) a new gown?

Even Douglas Howlett. Might not those three beautiful children—and the new one on the way—have been conceived in something other than love? Might Lorna's always-so-happy smile be for spectators only?

And how about Bryce Doolittle, the town's blacksmith? Might not the frail body of his wife, Carrie, secretly bear the marks of weekday abuse by one of Sunday's most pious worshipers?

What about Zachary Newhouse? Was he really so kind to his widowed mother—or was he the one who kept Grandma Rheba Newhouse from ordering the eyeglasses she so badly needed?

And what did Marnette know about Doc Britton? Was he really as good-humored as everyone thought? Might he not be surly and sullen at the dinner table, quick to criticize anything his daughters might do for him? Did the two sisters so willingly assist him on all those sick calls at his cabin, or did their father demand it?

Then there was the doctor's son. If Marnette had never heard any of those stories—or that terrible song—would she ever have suspected Drew Britton was capable of killing another man?

But she did know and she should be also glad to know that he had been secretly courting someone else.

She was glad, wasn't she?

❧

Marnette suddenly awoke to find Emilie—in barely enough daylight to be seen—setting a tray of food on the nightstand beside the bed.

"Grandma thought you should have some supper before you go."

In somewhat of a stupor from her accidental nap, apparently several hours long, Marnette asked her cousin, "Go where?"

"To the ball, of course."

Marnette abruptly sat up. "Emilie, you know I'm not going to the ball—and why!"

"But now you *have* something decent to wear," Emilie told her with a nod across the room.

Marnette squinted in the fading light. There, on the open door of the armoire, hung the pale blue challis gown that Emilie had so happily begun making and then so sadly stopped working on.

"But that's your gown," Marnette insisted.

"Not anymore," said Emilie. "Anyone can see it's too short."

"Too short?"

"For me," Emilie nodded. "But exactly right for you."

Marnette looked at the gown again. "Emilie—you didn't!"

"I most certainly did," she nodded again. "I cut off two whole inches. And now you have no reason for staying home."

She didn't bother adding that, by sacrificing her own gown, she herself had a good reason for staying home.

"Why?" Marnette demanded. "Why should you care whether or not I go to the Founders' Day ball?"

"Because I think it's time you stopped shying away from all the men," Emilie told her, heading for the door. "And it's not fair that my father should have to worry about supporting two old maids."

twelve

With her loosely-knit white summer shawl over her cousin's shortened blue challis gown, Marnette found herself on the front seat of the family buckboard, headed for the Founders' Day ball in the company of her Uncle Thad, a basket of seventy-two warm raspberry tarts, and her grandmother's Sunday umbrella.

Though the sky had merely remained overcast throughout the rest of the day, Ina Coulter was sure there would be more rain before the day's end. But even before she made that prediction, Marnette's grandmother had decided to stay home, preferring to spend a quiet evening with the Good Book over watching grown men and women "hopping around like frogs" on a dance floor. Nor did Theodore and Robert, having spent the day trying to win each and every one of the Founders' Day contests at the schoolyard, care to attend the "silly dance."

As they headed toward town in the clumsy wagon, several times Marnette's uncle counted his blessings, thankful that he had gotten his wheat harvested only two days before the rain. Even so, he was concerned that he had lost a whole day acting as one of the judges for the schoolyard contests. When they arrived at the new town hall, he told Marnette he was dropping her off so he could get to bed early and start on his neglected farm chores even earlier the next day.

"That'll be another contest," he chuckled. "All those young bucks jousting to take you home." He seemed not the least bit troubled that his unescorted niece would be fair game at the dance.

But it troubled Marnette. So much so, that she stood several moments outside the town hall's double doors before she was able to muster enough courage to walk in.

She lingered a while in the cloakroom, watching a number of couples out on the floor in a lively square dance, before she headed with the basket of tarts for the sweets table, as if it might be a port in a raging storm. There, she hoped, with her so obvious duties as hostess—lasting the whole night if she did not set all the sweets out at one time—she need not worry about anyone asking her to dance.

The truth was, she had yet to dance with any man and doubted she would know how. The only time she had come near to dancing had been back at the boarding school when Alma Veasley had been away on vacation and the acting mistress, the school's old maid music teacher, had invited some of the students from the nearby young men's academy for an evening of socializing: sipping punch and nibbling cookies to the strains of some popular Strauss waltzes played by the school's fledgling string quartet. Somehow it had ended with a number of the boys and girls dancing—sinful in the minds of some members of the school's board of directors—and the next day the errant spinster had been sacked.

Fear of sinning hadn't kept Marnette from dancing then. Nor did it now. It was pure and simple logic. Why would any young woman who had vowed never to marry willingly put herself in any young man's arms?

But logic had little to do with music. Not long after she had arranged the first set of sweets on the table, Marnette's feet were tapping to the sprightly rhythm of Tim Piper's fiddle, and she came dangerously close to wondering what would be the harm in one little dance.

But even though several of the town's unattached young men eventually came up to the table—some of them actually flirting with her—not one of them asked Marnette to dance.

Of course, there was one secretly attached young man whom

she had not expected would ask her to dance. But she was surprised in scanning the crowd (she told herself it was not in search of anyone in particular) to see Wilting Sunflower in Drew Britton's arms.

Marnette wondered why Wilting Sunflower would want to come to any Chappie Creek dance. Until she saw how, at every turn in her brother's arms, she kept stealing admiring glances at Tim Piper, smilingly playing his fiddle. Or was Marnette merely imagining that there might be something between Drew Britton's half sister and the new town clerk?

Did her brother suspect that the miller's son—honest as the day was long—might have less than honorable designs on his sister? Was that why the town constable was so relentlessly keeping guard over his sister, even between dances?

But what about the other girl, the one he was to eventually take home? Who was standing guard over her? Or was Drew Britton so secure in his secret courtship that he didn't care if his intended bride might be dancing with other men?

It shouldn't matter to her, what Drew Britton did or didn't mind, or that he had not come to the sweets table himself, but had sent the trader's grandson over for two glasses of punch.

As if to prove to herself that it didn't matter, Marnette turned and purposely focused on the whirling kaleidoscope of colorful ball gowns, as almost everyone but the town constable and his sister were out on the floor in a smooth-flowing waltz. The seamstress in her took some pleasure in the knowledge that at least nine of those gowns were the work of her own two hands.

There went Lorna Howlett, radiant in pink challis, whirling by in the arms of her handsome husband, Douglas. Marnette chided herself for ever having doubted their love—such radiance could only come from true happiness.

Next came Mattie Piper, in lemon-yellow chintz. With every turn in the arms of her high-stepping husband, Angus, Mattie stole proud glances at her fiddle-playing, town clerk son.

A half dozen more of Marnette's hand-sewn creations went billowing by the sweets table, among them a strawberry-pink poplin on Chester York's pretty wife, Hollis; a barred buttermilk muslin on Dolly Newhouse; and a soft lavender mull which, despite all of Marnette's take-ins and tucks, still hung like scarecrow's rags on the gaunt frame of Bryce Doolittle's work-worn wife, Carrie.

Gowns, gowns, and more full-skirted, gaily-tinted gowns— the fullest of which was the Widow Jaster's.

As Marnette had feared, Leah Jaster had not been thrilled with her choice of fabric, but with the many yards required for the extra full skirt, the green flowered chintz was the only thing Homer Farnsworth had had a big enough bolt of. Once resigned to the chintz, Leah had then made countless trips to the Coulter cabin for fittings, all in the bodice. She seemed determined to show the entire town that this not-yet-forty-year-old widow still had a youthful bosom.

Perhaps Leah didn't know that her still youthful face and figure, and still jet-black hair, were already begrudgingly admired by many a thick-waisted, early-graying Chappie Creek matron. But, if Leah Jaster was envied tonight, it was not because of her gown or her figure or her face. It was because of her handsome, youthful partner.

Watching them whirling about on the dance floor, Marnette thought that if Doc Britton's escorting the widow to the ball was a cure, it seemed to be working on both of them. Never had she seen Clay Britton's face so alive.

She wondered if there were not some women at the town hall tonight who were thinking the same thing as her cousin Emilie: that Doc Britton might be tempted to overlook Leah Jaster's razor-edged tongue enough to consider her as his third wife.

Her heart suddenly heavy for her stay-at-home cousin, Marnette turned away from all the dancers to see someone else whose status as a potential old maid probably would not be disputed: Abbie Britton, sitting in a far corner of the hall, talking with the Reverend Richard Humphries.

This was the pastor's first appearance at any kind of social event since his young wife had died, and Marnette wondered if that, too, might not be causing some female speculation: whether he had come tonight merely out of respect for the town's founders, or if the pastor might finally be ending his long period of mourning. Whatever, smiling and nodding his head every now and then, the pastor seemed to be enjoying his chat with the younger and plainer of Doc Britton's daughters.

Still not understanding why no one had asked her to dance—she would have refused, of course—Marnette turned to busy herself with setting some more sweets out on the table. She hadn't seen Doc Britton approaching and was totally surprised when he caught her hand after arranging several of her grandmother's tarts on the big tray.

"I think it's time the prisoner got some exercise."

It was a peculiar way of putting it, but Marnette knew she had just received her first invitation to dance.

"Don't worry," he added with a sly glint in his green eyes, "I have permission."

Marnette was sure he meant that his partner, now also talking with their pastor, had given him that permission.

"But I don't know how to dance," she told him.

"Nonsense. I've seen those tapping feet." And without further ado, the doctor led her out onto the floor.

Either he was a master at dancing himself or Marnette's feet did indeed have a mind of their own. She had no trouble at all in following the doctor as he gracefully maneuvered between the other couples in another lively waltz.

"The doctor was right, wasn't he?" he said with a little smile. "Knows a case of dancing feet when he sees them."

Marnette gave him a little smile in return. It occurred to her that in all her maneuvering to avoid his son the past three years, she had barely said any more than "hello" or "goodbye" to Doc Britton at either the trading post or at church. Sad, when he was the very one who had brought her to Chappie Creek. Even sadder, when she now knew her son-dodging had been for naught.

The doctor gave her a little whirl before asking her about another case: that of her cousin Emilie's absence from the ball tonight. "Nothing serious, I hope."

Marnette shook her head. "Just didn't feel up to it."

She wondered what Emilie would be feeling, now, if she were the rescued prisoner in the doctor's arms.

"No doubt all of this seems quite strange to you," he said after a little while. "Certainly nothing like back in Boston."

She supposed he meant his being the only one to have asked her to dance tonight when she was considered fair game. In Boston, a young woman would never even think of coming to any kind of mixed social event without a proper escort.

"Another of our town's curious little customs," he said wryly. "Or better yet, a sort of gentlemen's agreement." He gave her another little energetic spin. "But at least you'll have a buggy ride home."

It must have been the mystified look on his partner's face that led the waltzing doctor to his next diagnosis: "You don't have the faintest notion what I'm talking about—do you?"

She confirmed it with a shake of her head.

"Once a man stakes his claim, the others agree not to challenge it." He nodded toward his son, again out on the dance floor with his half sister. "And of course, being the town's official peace officer doesn't exactly hurt."

Marnette's dancing feet suddenly faltered. What was Doc Britton telling her? That her being the evening's only wallflower was because of some unwritten (and unchallenged) agreement between Drew Britton and the other unmarried men?

That the town constable had put a claim on her? But why? Why would any man claim one girl when he was courting another?

"I'm sure you're mistaken," she told his father.

"Anything but," he firmly shook his head. "Nor was I wrong three years ago. Knew it the minute you stepped off the stage that you were the girl my son was going to marry."

❧

The doctor had barely left her at the sweets table when Tim Piper announced the very last dance. And Marnette suddenly recalled what Emilie had told her about another Chappie Creek custom: being taken home by the one who claimed the last dance.

Hadn't the doctor just assured her that she would have a buggy ride home?

She knew any good hostess should also clean up the crumbs and empty the punch bowl before she left. But this one had a more urgent mission: getting out the door before someone else could cross the floor.

But Drew Britton had much longer legs than she did. And she was only halfway to the cloakroom when he caught her by the arm.

"I think this is my dance, Your Highness."

thirteen

If someone had asked Marnette Coulter who was the better dancer—the doctor or his son—she could not honestly have told them. Nor could she have said whether that last dance had been a polka or a waltz. If she had been aware of any rhythm at all, it was the pounding of her own heart.

For, being in Drew Britton's arms was worse than she had imagined. Worse yet was admitting she had ever imagined it.

He waltzed as he walked: a sure, self-confident step. And yet there was something akin to caution in the way he held her: as if she might indeed be a fragile china doll, apt to break at anything but the gentlest of handling.

If she had feared her partner's comments might also be too personal, she was in for another surprise.

"What do you think, now, of our new town hall?" he asked her after the second confident yet cautious twirl.

The truth was, Marnette had been so busy looking at—and trying not to look at—other couples on the floor, she had not paid too much attention to her surroundings. Even now she was too conscious of her own partner—the feel of his hand on her waist and her own hand in his—to truly appreciate what she saw: the coach-like lanterns mounted between the narrow French-paned windows and the crimson velvet drapes that had been hung—surely not by any of the men—on all ten of those windows.

Because she still did not trust her voice, Marnette merely gave her inquisitor a small shrug.

"Or maybe you agree with our pastor, that we should have built a decent church first."

"Or a separate schoolhouse."

She wasn't sure why she had said that. Especially when she hadn't yet presented Stuart Whittington's letter of resignation to the school board and didn't know if they would take his recommendation of her as his permanent replacement—or if she would even want to go on teaching, if they did.

"And when *is* the schoolmaster returning?" was her partner's next question, heavy with shared knowledge: that though Marnette had claimed to have gotten two letters, there really had been only one.

"Actually, he's not coming back at all," she admitted. "He's gotten married."

"Married? Old Muttonchops?"

"What's so strange about that?" she insisted, forgetting her own initial reaction had been the very same. "Look at your father—and Leah Jaster."

He glanced over his shoulder at his father and the once again smiling widow, also out on the floor for the evening's last dance. "That doesn't mean anything."

Marnette wished her cousin Emilie had been there to hear that. Indeed, she found it hard to believe that she herself was where she was: out on a dance floor in the arms of the man she had so carefully been avoiding the past three years.

As Drew adeptly maneuvered her between the other twirling couples, Marnette had to ask herself some soul-searching questions. If she truly wanted nothing to do with men, why had she so easily allowed Emilie to trick her into coming tonight?

And why—when she knew someone else would have to take her home—hadn't she simply left Grandma's tarts on the sweets table and gone back home with her Uncle Thad?

Why—when the town constable's father had told her just who would be taking her home—had she not bypassed the cloakroom and simply headed for the door?

"And what about you?" her partner asked.

Marnette's dancing feet suddenly failed her and he drew her closer before she actually tripped. She was suddenly conscious of the scent of home-made soap.

"You're going to stay on at the schoolhouse?"

"I don't know," she said truthfully. She thought of the schoolmaster's still unanswered letter. "I'm considering another offer."

She wasn't sure why she'd said that, when she knew in her heart that nothing and no one could ever entice her to go back to Boston. Unless it was to give Drew Britton an unwritten message: Marnette Coulter wasn't sitting around, waiting for some Chappie Creek "barbarian" to ask her to marry him.

If the town constable was surprised or worried, he didn't show it. Maybe he thought it was just another lie. Still, she thought he would at least ask her about her claimed offer.

But maybe all of his questions had merely been polite conversation while dancing. Maybe his claiming the last dance didn't mean anything at all, and his father had been totally wrong in his three-year-old prognosis regarding his son's heart.

Maybe it had merely been wishful thinking on the doctor's part. Having been the one who had brought Marnette Coulter to Chappie Creek, he might have hoped that someone might save her from becoming an old maid, saddling his good friend Thad Coulter with yet a third woman to support with his wheat farming.

Whatever, the two young people finished the evening's last dance in silence. When the town constable led her toward the cloakroom, Marnette knew his father was right about at least one thing: She had herself a ride home.

&

There had been only a few other umbrellas in the cloakroom when Marnette had hung hers, along with her summer shawl, on one of the hooks. Most of the crowd at the town hall, not having had the benefit of Ina Coulter's second accurate forecast, had not suspected Founders' Day would end in a four-wheeled race for home in the rain.

Even if she had known, Leah Jaster probably would not have been too concerned, since she had come to the ball in one of the few closed buggies among all those wagons hitched to the trees in the adjacent schoolyard. How was she to know that someone else would be going home in Doc Britton's black house-call buggy, and that she would be taken home by the doctor—along with his two unattached daughters—in the family's open buckboard?

"The merry widow doesn't look so merry now," Drew chuckled as he got into the buggy seat beside Marnette after untethering his father's mare. "Probably'll give my father a good tongue-lashing all the way home."

Marnette caught the outraged look on Leah Jaster's wet face as the Britton buckboard splashed by.

"But, I doubt promising to bring her back dry was part of the bargain," Drew added.

Marnette gave her driver a questioning look. Though the past two Sundays she had overheard some of the women's churchyard whisperings about the doctor and the widow, not one of them had referred to the surprising Founders' Day coupling as a bargain.

"She's the one who asked him, you know," he said, taking the reins. "And being one of the few real gentlemen in town, my father couldn't refuse."

Marnette did not miss his dry reference to her own claimed shortage of gentlemen in Chappie Creek. She might have made a little face, if she hadn't been inwardly smiling at the good news for her cousin, Emilie, that Doc Britton, too, had been tricked into coming tonight.

Though of all that night's revelers they had the longest ride home, Marnette's last-minute escort seemed in no big rush to get going. He waited until most of the wagons had disappeared on the muddy road before he flicked the reins.

Maybe he was simply concerned about the mare's ability to safely navigate in such a torrential rain, for once on the road, they moved at slightly more than a possum's pace. If it were merely to give them more time to talk, he lost at least two minutes of that time in searching for the right words.

Did Marnette want to hear what the doctor's son might eventually say? What if his father wasn't wrong? What would *she* say?

When Drew's continued silence began to feel uncomfortable, she decided to break it herself. "Both of your sisters seemed to be having a good time tonight. Especially Wilting Sunflower."

She was immediately sorry she had said that, fearing he might interpret it as her being piqued at his leaving her alone at the sweets table while he spent the evening dancing with his sister. Or even, that she might know anything about a "gentlemen's agreement" between him and the other single men.

"It's the first time she's ever come to any of the dances," he nodded. "And I knew no one else would ask her to dance."

When Marnette said nothing he gave her a wry chuckle. "I'd really have had my hands full, if there had been two."

It was impossible for Marnette not to respond to that. "Two?"

"Twins do run in my family, you know."

She merely nodded, but she was thinking that any woman who married Drew Britton probably would also have twins.

"And my father still isn't sure Wilting Sunflower didn't have a twin sister—or brother."

"How could he possibly *not* know?"

"Well, you see—" They had come to the fork in the road, and he turned the buggy onto the one leading to her uncle's farm. "They were still living in the Indian village, and he was away with a hunting party when the baby—or babies—came about a month early. His wife was already dead when he got back, and one of the other squaws was nursing my sister. My father thinks they may have drowned the other baby."

Marnette sucked in her breath. "Why would they do that?"

Drew waited until the buggy had rolled into and out of one of the deeper puddles in the road. "Some tribes have some really strange beliefs, Marnie. Some believe that a woman is supposed to have only one child at a time, and if ever there are two, the second child is thought to be an evil spirit."

"That's terrible."

"Not to them—at least not back then." He glanced in the direction of the Indian village. "That's one of the reasons why—besides bringing them white man's medicine—my father and my two sisters so often go out to the village. To try to preach the gospel, as well. I suspect that's what Abbie was up to tonight—trying to talk the Reverend Humphries into going out there, too. After all, the red man needs saving just as much as all those other white folks he preaches to on his monthly circuit ride."

That Drew Britton would so easily talk about things like the gospel and salvation gave Marnette some unexpected food for thought. She had often wondered at his showing up at church every Sunday, especially when so many other young men in town thought religion was only for women and children.

"I didn't know Abbie was going out to the village, too."

Drew didn't say what he could have: that if Marnette Coulter hadn't stayed away from his sister's monthly sewing bees—and all those other Chappie Creek sociables and barn dances—she might have learned even more. Things like unwritten gentlemen's agreements and who might be secretly courting whom.

"But I sometimes wonder if my father doesn't think they were right."

"Who?" she asked him, having lost his train of thought along with her own. "Right about what?"

"The Indians, and the second baby being a devil." He gave her a little grin. "Maybe that's why this twin spent so much time in the woodshed."

She tried to ignore the vivid picture in her mind of Drew Britton as a naughty little tow-headed boy needing a trip to the woodshed.

He gave her a sideways glance. "That's beautiful."

"What is?"

"You—smiling. I thought maybe you didn't know how."

Marnette turned her face to the muddy road. He was right: Not once since they had met had she ever smiled at Drew Britton. She certainly hadn't meant to smile at him tonight.

Here she was, so casually riding and talking in the rain with the man she had so carefully avoided for over three years. The whole thing was crazy, especially after what his father had told her tonight.

"Anyway," Drew went on, as if there had been no break at all in his on-the-road family history, "that's why my father decided to go back East and study for doctoring—so he could bring real medicine back to his wife's village. It was in Boston that he met my mother, and I'm sure you've heard all the stories about her."

Marnette didn't answer. She hated to admit she paid any attention to what she heard at the trading post. Then she might also have to admit she had heard all those stories about him— and that fatal day in the woods.

"Well, it wasn't anything like what people say," Drew added soberly.

Marnette still did not respond. She didn't want to hear the real story behind Jessica Britton's death—not from her own son. She was sorry he had told her as much as he had about himself and his family, for somehow that seemed more intimate than being in his arms.

But Drew seemed determined to go on. "Abbie and I were

only babies ourselves when it happened. But my father told us the whole story when we were old enough to understand."

"You don't have to tell it to me," Marnette said, hoping that would be enough to discourage him.

"But I want you to know."

Drew slowed the mare's pace even more, as if to give himself enough time to tell Marnette Coulter the whole story.

"It all began about a year after they moved back here from Boston and she learned that his first wife had been an Indian."

"You mean he never told her?"

Drew shook his head. "He didn't think it mattered. But it did. So much that she wouldn't sleep with him anymore—though she was already expecting again."

Again Marnette turned her face to the road, fearful that in the glow of the buggy's lanterns, he might see on her face a vision not of the doctor sleeping alone, but rather of his grown-up son still doing the same.

"She said it was a sin for a white man to marry an Indian—an even worse sin that they should have a child. She almost went crazy when my father told her he wanted to bring Wilting Sunflower home to Chappie Creek."

Somewhere along the road it had stopped raining.

"Every time my father went out to the village, he could see he had made a mistake in leaving Wilting Sunflower there, thinking the women would take good care of her. He only had to look at her to know she wasn't getting enough to eat. It seemed some of those Indian women also thought it might be a sin to mix red blood with white, and they never really accepted Wilting Sunflower as one of their own. He suspected the village dogs got to the scraps before she did."

Marnette made a little sympathetic sound, hardly a reaction to discourage any storyteller. But would anything have kept Drew Britton from finishing his unhappy tale?

"There was someone else in the village not getting enough

to eat—an old widowed squaw who wasn't able to do her share of the women's work anymore. My father—knowing he couldn't bring my sister back to Chappie Creek—struck a bargain with the old woman. She could come to our smokehouse whenever she wanted and take whatever she wanted, so long as she shared what she took with Wilting Sunflower.

"It wasn't long before my mother found out about it," continued Drew. "One night when the rest of us were asleep, she sneaked out to the smokehouse, splashed a can of kerosene on it, tossed a bucket of live coals at it, and burned the whole thing down. She didn't know—until she heard her screams—that the old woman was still inside."

"Oh, Drew!" Marnette gasped. Only later would she realize it was the first time she had ever spoken his name.

"As much as my mother hated the Indians," he went on, "she knew she had done a terrible thing. When her baby was stillborn the next day, she was sure it was a punishment from God. And our pastor back then, with all his preaching about God's wrath, made her all the more certain."

The buggy was now going so slowly, it was almost not moving.

"Every day she got worse—so burdened with guilt that she couldn't get out of bed during the day."

Marnette could easily believe that. She herself had been so shackled with shame after learning the truth about her mother that for three whole days she had not been able to come down for meals or classes.

"My father knew she was getting up at night and wandering, in just her nightgown, through the woods. For a whole month he slept by the fire with one eye open so he could follow her and make sure she came back safely."

The buggy had stopped moving, and in the growing glow of moonlight, Marnette thought she saw Leo and Lorna Chappie's old cabin among the trees.

"One night my father was so exhausted, he slept straight through till morning, only to find there'd been a big blizzard during the night—so bad it took the town two whole days to dig out. It was on the third day that he found my mother up on the hill .. ."

He nodded back toward Massacre Hill.

"Frozen solid on their dead baby's grave."

"Oh, Drew!"

Marnette kept her hands tightly clasped in her lap to keep from trying to comfort the doctor by touching his son.

"Not too long after that," Drew said, as if to end his story, "my father brought Wilting Sunflower home to live with us."

Once again Marnette turned her face to the road. She knew there was more to the story, that there was another tragic chapter in Wilting Sunflower's life.

"I'm sure there are a lot of other sad stories that could be told," he said with a little nod toward the old Chappie cabin, lit up in the full glow of the moon. "Especially if that old cabin could speak."

Marnette had seen the cabin countless times in the light of day, passing it every time she came into town. It was like most of the other small cabins she had seen on her trip west with Drew Britton's father—the stone fireplace chimney almost dwarfing the little log house.

"You'd probably learn that pioneering wasn't as romantic as you had the kids play it up on the stage this morning."

She was too relieved at the shift in his mood to take any offense at his criticism of her pantomimed history of Chappie Creek. She wondered, though, why he had chosen to stop at the Chappies' long-abandoned cabin.

"Nice and private," he said with another nod toward the cabin, "tucked away behind those trees and with the creek just behind it. A nice little place for a young couple just starting out."

Marnette was sure he meant Leo and Lorna Chappie, for they had been married only a year when they had come west. Though she knew Leo had built the cabin quickly to serve merely as a shelter for Lorna and their new baby before he began clearing the land for their first crop, Marnette said, "Yes, but you'd think he would have made it a bit bigger."

"Fireplace is a real work of art," Drew said, as if not having heard her. "And the well—that still works, too."

"I can't understand why he didn't later add on to it—"

"Take no time at all to add a couple rooms—especially if a man was already handy with an axe and a saw."

"—Especially after they had all those other children."

She thought she heard her driver give out a frustrated sigh before he flicked the reins. When the buggy began rolling again, Marnette had the feeling that the schoolmarm had again disappointed the town's most handy builder in her grading of a certain building in town.

Though he said nothing at all the rest of the way, Marnette's driver still seemed in no big hurry to get her home. She herself was in no rush for the buggy ride to end. She couldn't convince herself that the town constable had gone to the trouble of claiming the last dance merely to stop and speculate about the old Chappie Cabin while taking her home.

When they finally reached the cutoff to her uncle's cabin and Drew again reined the buggy to a stop, Marnette was surprised at the question he abruptly asked her.

"Those books you've been getting from Boston—you're sure they're from him? Stuart Whittington?"

"Of course I'm sure."

But hadn't she begun to wonder, after she had gotten his letter at the trading post? Wondered about the manner in which all four of the books had been addressed-in square, masculine letters proclaimed—*To the Chappie Creek Schoolmarm*. They didn't in the least look like the schoolmaster's flowery script

on the pages of his long letter and the envelope addressed to
Miss Marie Antoinette Coulter.

Even before she had gotten the schoolmaster's letter,
shouldn't Marnette have known that Stuart Whittington—such
a master of the King's English, would never have addressed
any female school teacher as "schoolmarm"?

Nor was she truly thinking, now, when she asked Drew
Britton, "If not Mister Whittington—who else?"

"Maybe a not-so-secret admirer," he said, shifting on the
buggy seat so he was facing her. "Some men bring sweets,
others flowers. Another man might court a girl with books."

Though the rain had long ago stopped, Marnette found herself drawing her knit summer shawl even closer. She barely
recognized her own voice.

"But I didn't have any beaus back East—I was only sixteen
when I left Boston."

"A very sweet and soft sixteen," he nodded. "And I didn't
mean Boston."

Marnette clutched the shawl closer yet, as if it might keep
him from hearing the sudden pounding of her heart. What was
Drew Britton telling her—that *he* had sent her those four romantic books? That his father had been right? That she was
the girl he had been secretly courting?

> *And the sunlight clasps the earth*
> *And the moonbeams kiss the sea;*
> *What is all this sweet work worth*
> *If thou kiss not me?*

When he moved closer yet, she was sure his next move would
be to take her in his arms. But again she was surprised.

"I bought the old Chappie cabin, Marnette," he said slowly
and deliberately, as if to give her time for it to finally sink in—
all he had said earlier about the fireplace and the well and

adding some rooms. "I bought it for us."

She opened her mouth as if to protest, but he cut her short.

"Don't tell me any more lies, Marnie. I know you love me."

"No."

Even as she said it, Marnette knew it was another lie. But the biggest lie was the one she had so long been telling herself. No matter what Drew Britton had done when he himself had been only sixteen, he had carved his name on her heart the very day they had met.

"We've wasted too much time already, Marnie," he told her. "I don't want to waste any more."

And he didn't.

Nor did she. For when he took her in his arms, she met him more than halfway.

And in their kiss, her mouth was as eager as his.

fourteen

Chappie Creek's "two washdays summer" finally ended, and no one was more relieved than Homer Farnsworth. Some of the families had used up their homemade bars of soap, and he was tired of telling the women that his order of factory-made laundry soap had not yet come in.

But there was something the trader never got tired of telling anyone who would listen, and he was having trouble deciding that late September morning which story to tell first: the one about Leah Jaster putting her farm up for sale or the one about Marnette Coulter coming into the post shortly after to order the satin for her wedding gown.

Of course, the one about the Coulter girl really wasn't news, not after Drew Britton had broken all those other girls' hearts the night of the Founders' Day ball, and two days later had begun working like a crazy man, himself, trying to turn the old Chappie cabin into a three-room castle for his intended bride.

And hadn't the schoolmarm herself told him the most surprising story of all: about the prissy bachelor schoolmaster also getting married? Some folks, though, were more disappointed than surprised. At least Stu Whittington would never have goaded all those parents into sending their girls to school this fall, when they all knew it was just a waste of time.

Of course, the trader would never admit to anyone but himself what a blessing it had been that his good wife, Emma, had been able to read and write, and how hard it was to run the store since she was gone.

He didn't know what he would have done if it hadn't been

for his orphaned grandson, Jonathan, helping him write the orders and read the labels on all those cans and sacks of food when they came out by wagon every other month. And when the monthly stagecoach came in with the mail, the boy not only sorted the letters and packages, he also ran them out to their receivers the very same day.

The only time Homer had had to deliver the mail himself was that time when the boy had been down with the grippe. Luckily there had been only one letter from Boston, addressed to "M.A. Coulter."

"M.A." spelled "Ma," didn't it? And because there was only one "Ma Coulter" in Chappie Creek, he had driven the delivery wagon out to the farm and personally handed the letter to Ina Coulter. It must have been something really important, for though she never wrote any letter back, for at least half the year after that, Ina Coulter had been the first one at the post, waiting for the mail on the monthly stage. There might have been a story worth telling there, Homer thought, but that had been almost three years ago.

Even the stories he could tell today would not raise that many eyebrows. The only news that might have truly surprised anyone would have been Doc Britton's half-Indian daughter also coming into the post for the makings of a wedding gown.

Everyone knew that Wilting Sunflower—should any man be desperate enough to want to marry her—would have had to order something other than white satin. She had lived among the good Christian folks of Chappie Creek long enough to know she had forfeited the privilege of wearing white.

Maybe the town constable's little lady-love would also end up wearing something other than white satin. Did anyone really believe she had spent that Saturday with him at the old cabin merely measuring for curtains and deciding on what furniture he was going to make for her once the cabin was done?

Wouldn't all those other women just love to hear a story like that about Ina Coulter's snooty Boston-bred granddaughter?

☙

Ina Coulter watched from the cabin window as Marnette, toting her worn-out carpetbag, headed for the schoolhouse. Yes, there was a definite spring to her step. This morning she had been softly humming as she had gotten dressed and had then sat dreamily smiling throughout breakfast. Sure signs of a girl gone sappy with love.

There must have been signs before, and Ina chided herself for having missed them. She prided herself on always having her ear to the ground, especially when it came to her family.

Of course, there was one sign she had not missed, had seen on the girl's face the very day she'd arrived: that Marnette was not telling the truth about her mother. So many times Ina had been tempted to tell her that she knew, that she had learned the truth not too long after Marnette had come to Chappie Creek.

Wasn't that another of God's little tender mercies—that Homer Farnsworth should have delivered that despicable letter when Ina had been all alone at the cabin?

"Got a letter for you," was all the trader had said, so she had never bothered to look at the name on the envelope. She was already into the second poisonous paragraph before she realized the letter was meant for Marnette.

She might be a simple prairie woman, but Ina Coulter knew blackmail when she saw it. And as she stood watching the letter turn to ashes in the fireplace, she came near to wishing the same fate for its writer—A.V.—who had not, of course, signed his (or her?) full name.

She was sure that she had done the right thing in burning the letter, for there had never been any more. Still, she knew she had taken a serious gamble that the person back in Boston would never carry out his or her threat to spread the story about Marnette's mother throughout the town. A story many other young women, envious of Marnette's beauty and bearing, would delight in hearing.

Ina watched from the window as Marnette made the bend in the dirt road. What a burden for the girl to carry all these years, and how many lies she had had to tell to hide her shame.

But at least those frightful nightmares were getting fewer and farther between. Ina probably should thank the Lord that the girl had never followed her advice to "talk out" those dreams. She was sure, now, that those dreams were about her father and that Marnette had lied about him, too.

Well, God bless the girl for that. Even before he had been spirited off to sea, Ina had known her whiskey-sodden son would come to a bad end. She wouldn't mind going to her grave never knowing the torments Thomas Coulter had put his wife and daughter through before he had come to that end.

Ina turned from the window with a deep sigh just as Emilie came in from the barn.

"We finally found it, Grandma—behind the pickle barrel."

"I knew it had to be out there somewhere," Ina nodded.

What Emilie and her father had finally found was Ina's disassembled and burlap-wrapped loom—the only thing, besides her clothes, her two prized pewter plates, and her beloved Boston rocker, that she had brought with her on her own journey west to come live with her older son those many years ago.

"Pa wants to know if he should bring it in and set it up now."

"No," Ina shook her head. "Tell him to set it up for me out there in the barn." She had a ready answer for Emilie's doubtful look. "We're going to have ourselves a real Indian summer before winter sets in, and I should be done weaving long before then."

Emilie Coulter had lived through enough of her grandmother's weather forecasts not to argue about this latest one.

"Besides, Marnie's never once gone out to the barn—and this way the blanket will be a surprise."

Emilie smiled. "The quilt, too, I hope." She and the other

women were jointly making a patchwork quilt at Abbie Britton's monthly sewing bees: a wedding gift for Abbie's brother and his January bride. Ina had been invited to join in the project, but she had insisted on making her own gift. A quilt was fine, but a thick Indian blanket under it would be even warmer for a couple beginning their married life in the dead of winter.

When Emilie went back to the barn, Ina silently thanked the Lord for yet another favor: that her hand-woven blanket would not be a going away gift, that Marnette had not taken Stuart Whittington up on his offer for her to come back to Boston. Of course, Ina couldn't tell anyone about that, because then she would have to admit she had read the letter she had found tucked away among Marnette's petticoats in the dresser she shared with Emilie. She never would have read it if she hadn't feared it might—even after so many years—be a second letter from that would-be blackmailer in Boston.

Ina sighed again. So many secrets for one tired old woman to have to carry. Of course, the biggest secret she had ever been burdened with was the one Wilting Sunflower had tearfully shared that spring day when they had accidentally met up on Massacre Hill—the hardest to carry whenever she heard the children singing that dreadful song about the girl's brother.

She was glad Marnette had not let that song—and all those stories about him at the trading post—keep her from seeing what a truly fine young man Drew Britton was.

But if someone had asked Ina Coulter a few months ago which of her granddaughters might be in love with the doctor's son, she would not have said Marnette. For only when she had gone into that worrisome funk those weeks before Founders' Day, had Emilie Coulter ever missed one of Abbie Britton's monthly sewing bees.

fifteen

Marnette followed her nineteen students toward the little clearing in the woods where they had been eating their lunch the entire week. She wished she could bottle up the lovely Indian summer days and store them away for the winter. It seemed the Creator (would she ever be able to call him "Father"?) was sitting back on His heels to admire His own handiwork—the growing all done, and the greens slowly mellowing into crimson or gold. This October He seemed to have outdone Himself. Or was that because she was looking at God's world with happier eyes?

Wasn't that a miracle, that Marnette Coulter should spring from her bed every morning with a sense of joy? She still found it hard to believe that in three short months she and Drew Britton would be married. Sooner, if he was able to get all the work at the cabin done before then. He might already have been done with the cabin itself if he hadn't insisted that the two new rooms he was adding should also be made of logs. To preserve the rustic beauty of the town's most revered historical landmark, he had told her, adding that poetry was not merely found in the pages of a book. There could be poetry in a man's building.

But what made this poetic builder's progress even slower was that he had not asked any of the other men to help him. Indeed, his would be the only home in Chappie Creek that had not gone up with the help of every able-bodied man in town.

Because Drew Britton had broken with this honored prairie tradition, his work on the old Chappie cabin caused somewhat derisive speculation around the stove at the trading post.

Marnette knew this because she had overheard some of the old-timers' talk the day she had come into the post for more thread, and they hadn't known she was there.

"Did you see those logs? Flat as a pancake."

They were talking about Drew's extra labor in cutting the inside of the logs flat so Marnette could put up some samplers or dried flowers to make the cabin homier.

Not only that, but Drew had also bought the four windows that had been left over after the town hall had been built, and each of the cabin's new rooms had two French-paned windows that could actually be opened.

Marnette didn't mind the old men's comments about the town constable "building a castle for his little uppity Boston princess" when he should be patrolling the town, on the alert for any law-breakers. But she wanted to crawl under the yard goods counter when they made those other crude remarks about that Saturday when she had been alone with Drew at the cabin. Hadn't her grandmother cautioned her not to stay too long? Shouldn't she have known better?

From that day on, Marnette made sure that the only time she and Drew were together was when he came to dinner at her uncle's cabin or to lunch at the schoolhouse when there were no less than thirty-eight chaperoning eyes.

But even though she had been alone with him only that one day, Marnette had learned much about the man with whom she would spend the rest of her life. While she had been surprised at his romantic philosophy about building onto the cabin, she was even more surprised to learn that he was such a perfectionist. But didn't that explain why no one ever complained when it took him so long to make a new armoire or washstand? Everyone knew the piece would be perfect.

Marnette had at first felt cheated that, fearful of any more wagging tongues, she could not be alone with Drew at the cabin while he would be working on their new furniture. But that had been before he had begun coming to the schoolhouse at lunchtime. And, though those brief visits were anything but private, she had come to cherish them, for she found herself learning even more about this man who soon would be her husband.

For one thing, he seemed to love the way the youngest of the children all rushed at him when he showed up and the way they wolfed down their lunches, knowing what was in store for them once they were done. He always made them wait until he had eaten his own lunch before he would slowly reach into his pocket for his jackknife and some small piece of wood.

Marnette knew, now, that it wasn't merely the town constable's whittling that always attracted those children on the trading post steps. It was the stories that went along with the carving. Stories that only a man who loved children would be able to tell.

Today, even before she reached the forest clearing, the happy shouts of some of the children told Marnette their storyteller was already there. When she saw him sitting on the fallen log, she herself had a hard time not rushing at him. There was no one more eager than she for the town constable to finish his lunch and make that slow, teasing reach into his pocket.

He always came with a piece of wood that was already crudely carved into a hint of whatever it was to be insisting that the wood was exactly the way he had found it.

The piece usually turned out to be a bird or some other small woodland creature that would, as he deftly whittled, become the subject of the day's story. But only after he asked the children to guess what it was going to be.

Today his piece of wood looked more like the beginnings of a little doll, and Nancy Mae Cunningham was the first to guess it.

"But what kind of a doll?" Drew asked her.

"A china doll?" she said hopefully.

"No—but that's certainly close," he said with a sidelong glance at Marnette, beside him on the fallen log. And she couldn't suppress a little smile, recalling the day he had called her just that. Again she was sorry for all those years she had wasted, running away from him. Especially when she saw the calluses on his palms, evidence of all his long and loving work for her out at their cabin.

"I think—" he now told the children, slowly turning the little piece of wood over in his hands, "—this one has a little fairy princess inside."

"Aw, that's a lot of hogwash," said Tommy Sutter.

There was only one story Tommy wanted to hear, but every time he asked about the shooting in the woods, the town constable turned deaf. Nor would he explain why, as the town's keeper of law and order, he didn't carry a gun.

"Oh, hush up, Tommy!" said one of the girls as if she, too, knew Drew Britton was just fooling and she didn't care.

"There's no such things as fairies," the boy insisted. If he couldn't hear the story he wanted to hear, he wanted it known that he considered anything else pure nonsense.

"That's where you're wrong," the town constable told him. "I know a man who met a fairy princess—right here in Chappie Creek."

"Really?" said Nancy Mae, her eyes as wide as those of the other nine girls. "A good fairy?"

"For sure," he solemnly nodded. "But still about half a pint wicked."

The girls were all silent, as if trying to envision that: a fairy princess with half a pint of wickedness. Their teacher was also silent as she reached into her carpetbag for one of her precious Boston books, pretending she wasn't the least bit interested, either, in such noontime nonsense.

"What did she look like?" one of the other girls dared to ask.

"Well," said their storyteller, beginning to chip away at his pre-formed piece of wood, "she had a very pretty face and beautiful long, dark hair. Only sometimes she rolled it into a little bird's nest so nobody could be sure just how long it really was."

"You mean like Teacher's?" asked yet another girl.

"Yes," he nodded with a sidelong glance at his partner on the log. "Exactly like that. And she had this snooty little nose that she kept way up in the air." He demonstrated with his own lean, aristocratic nose. "So nobody could tell she was looking at them."

Opening her book—it didn't matter which one—Marnette thought of that sweltering day at the schoolhouse when she was sure Drew had caught her looking at him, in all his builder's bareness, from the window.

"But if she was so pretty," asked Melanie Newhouse, "how did the man know she was wicked?"

"For one thing," Drew said, going back to his whittling, "she would tell big whopping lies."

And again Marnette thought back to the lies she had told Drew about Stuart Whittington, right here on this very same log.

"But the wickedest thing about this little fairy princess was her eyes," said the children's storyteller, holding his little wooden doll up as if trying to decide where to carve next. "Big, brown, doe-baby eyes that could make a man's heart do a complete somersault."

"Oh!" said two of the girls in unison, as if able to actually see such anatomical magic.

"But that wasn't the worst thing she could do to a man's heart," Drew said, making a sudden gouging cut into the piece of wood. No one dared say anything, for fear he meant cutting the poor man's heart right out of him.

"She could take it and twist it." He did exactly that with his piece of wood. "Just like warm taffy."

"Oh," said one of the girls, "that must have really hurt."

"Sometimes it did," he said with yet another glance at their supposedly reading schoolmarm. "But he always went back for more."

"That man must have been really stupid," said Tommy. The boy had not been too bright himself, in admitting he had gotten caught up in the town constable's little lunchtime fable.

"But that's how much power this little fairy princess had," said Drew.

"Probably a spell," nodded one of the girls knowledgeably.

"It certainly was," Drew said with still another glance at the "reader" beside him on the log. "Lasted for almost three years—until he finally figured out how to break it."

There was total silence in the clearing, as if even the twittering birds were waiting to hear how the poor man had broken the princess' spell.

"He kissed her."

All nine of the girls gasped, and all but one of the boys made sick-to-their-stomach faces.

"What'd I tell you?" said the doubting Thomas in their midst. "I knew it was all hogwash!"

But at least one of the girls was not too shocked to want to know the results of that kiss. "And what did that do—take away all of her power?"

"No," said the woodcarver with the softest of glances at their schoolmarm. "As a matter of fact, it gave her even more."

❧

The children ran on ahead while their teacher and the town constable slowly followed them back to the schoolhouse.

"How did you like my little story?" he asked her before they got to his father's mare, tied to one of the schoolyard trees.

Marnette thought of that other love story she had read aloud to her students that very morning, mostly for the benefit of the seven new girls. Three of them had cried at Romeo and Juliet's tragic ending.

"I would have liked it more," she told her own lover, "if it had ended with their living happily ever after."

"They will, Marnie," he assured her, taking her in his arms. "That's a promise."

And when the woodcarver kissed his little fairy princess, she didn't care if the whole world might be watching.

sixteen

It came on the last stagecoach before winter, and the trader's grandson delivered it as Marnette was closing up the schoolhouse for the day. Though the sky had been promising the season's first snow, Marnette lingered a while longer to read Stuart Whittington's second letter.

My Dear Marie Antoinette,

I cannot fully express my disappointment at your not answering my first letter. Yet I am hoping you have delayed your response only to seriously consider my proposal that you come and live with me and my little family in Boston.

Let me assure you, my dear, that the offer still stands. Indeed, your serving us as governess is even more urgent, now, since God has seen fit to bless our happy union with another child, and my sweet wife, Norma, now in her fourth month, finds caring for the three girls every day becoming more difficult. I must confess that I, myself, am little help to her since I did find a new teaching position in this historic city—at none other than your own alma mater, the Beacon Hill Academy for Young Women.

I must admit, though, that my securing the position was no simple matter since, as I am sure you know, that institution—being widely known

*for its excellent deportmental training—has a
board of directors most steadfast in their
solicitude for the virtue of the young ladies in
their charge. For them to even consider employ-
ing a teacher of the opposite gender was an
historic event in itself.*

*Knowing this beforehand, I came to the
interview with the headmistress armed with what
I was certain were two strong points in my favor:
the fact that I already was married with three
daughters of my own, and my acquaintance—
indeed cherished friendship—with one of the
academy's finest alumnae.*

*You can imagine my chagrin when the woman
told me there was no record of the school's ever
having any student bearing your name. Needless
to say, I left the office of the headmistress in a
most befuddled state. I would perhaps have been
forever mystified if I had not been approached
on my way out of the building by the school's
most amiable Irish cook who, having somehow
eavesdropped on the interview, told me the
headmistress was "lying through her tea-stained
teeth."*

*This information, of course, only put me in a
deeper quandary and, though I had come to the
academy seeking employment, my quest was
suddenly changed into solving the mystery of
why Miss Alma Veasley would want to deny your
six years as a student at the school. I never
suspected what a Pandora's box I was to open
with my amateur detective work.*

*I learned that the headmistress was correct in
there being no written record of your enrollment,*

simply because she had been slipping your monthly tuition into her own pocket.

That was not the woman's only nefarious enterprise. She was also engaged—by virtue of opening and resealing the other students' mail— in what could only be termed blackmail.

I did not delve too deeply into any of her victims' secrets—for I am sure they have already suffered enough—but I do know she was successful in one particular case because the young woman had not been solicitous of her own virtue on at least one weekend at home, and that to remedy the situation, her father had secured the physician's services of another student's father.

To make an already too long story short, my dear, the Beacon Hill Academy for Young Women now has a new headmistress, along with a gentleman teacher of American Literature who still hopes with all his heart that in the spring, when the stagecoach will again be running, one of the school's former students will be on it.

Meanwhile, I pray that God will bless Chappie Creek with a not too harsh winter and that your fourth (and hopefully last) Christmas out on the prairie will be a most happy one.

> *Affectionately,*
> *Stuart P. Whittington, Esq.*

P.S. The academy also will eventually have a new cook since, beginning the first of the year, Katie Sullivan—"tired of trying to make turnips

> *taste like T-bone"—will be working her culinary*
> *magic in the kitchen of the Boston Whittingtons.*

Toting her schoolmarm's carpetbag in the winter's first feathery snowfall, Marnette slowly headed for home, mulling over Stuart Whittington's second letter.

While not surprised about Miss Veasley's extracurricular activities, Marnette was stunned to learn that there were skeletons in the closets of those other girls' upright Boston families and that she was not the only student at the academy with an unsavory secret.

It suddenly occurred to Marnette that the devious headmistress could have attempted to blackmail her, too. After all, Miss Veasley could easily have learned her whereabouts from the friend with whom Doc Britton had come to the school that fateful rainy day.

What would Marnette have done if Alma Veasley *had* sent her a letter, threatening to tell someone in Chappie Creek about her mother's shameful "business"? How, as merely a once-in-a-while seamstress and temporary schoolteacher, would she have found enough money to buy the woman's silence?

What if she *hadn't* been able to send enough money? And what if the woman *had* somehow spread the ugly story throughout the town?

Would Sarah Humphries ever have invited Marnette to tea? Would the pastor have been so happy to have her as a member of his flock? Would any of those Sunday worshipers want to sit in the same church with her?

She had to wonder, too, if Stuart Whittington would have thought of leaving her in charge of the schoolhouse, or if any of those parents would have allowed even their roughneck boys to attend school.

Would she ever have taken a single stitch for anyone but herself? Would any of the women have wanted to be seen in even a flour sack apron made by Cynthia Coulter's daughter?

And what about her own family? If Emilie knew the truth, would she still want to sleep in the same bed with her? Might Grandma Coulter have long ago sent her packing, as her other grandmother had? And where would Marnette have gone if she had?

And what about Drew Britton? Would a man who had killed another man for violating his sister want to marry the daughter of a whore?

That was the most troubling thought of all, troubling Marnette all the more the closer she came to the old Chappie cabin where Drew was this very moment waiting to take her the rest of the way home. She had resolved never to tell anyone, especially him, any more lies. But wasn't it a lie not to tell her future husband the truth about her past? Could she ever hope to be happy as Drew Britton's wife, forever haunted by both the lie and the fear that he might someday find out?

By the time she had reached the cabin, Marnette not only was covered with snow, she was determined to tell Drew the truth. But she almost lost that resolve when she saw him heading for the buckboard waiting at the new hitching post he had set into the ground only that day.

"Drew, there's something I have to tell you," she told him, staying his hand on the reins once he had gotten onto the driver's seat beside her.

"Can't it wait until I get you home?"

She supposed he was concerned about the snowfall, getting to look more like a blizzard every minute. Or maybe he was fearful that her grandmother might be cross at their being so late, since this was one of the nights Drew was to stay for dinner at her uncle's cabin.

"No, I want to tell you now, before I change my mind," she said, taking a deep and tremulous breath. "Because it might change *your* mind about marrying me."

He turned on the seat to slowly take her in his arms. "Marnie, there is only one thing you could ever tell me that would change my mind. That you don't love me."

Even if he hadn't closed her mouth in that long, breathless kiss, Marnette could never have truthfully told him that.

seventeen

No one had to ask Ina Coulter if Chappie Creek was going to have a white Christmas. The town had been under a blanket of white since Thanksgiving and now, on Christmas Eve, they were having another blizzard.

Snow on Christmas, Ina cheerfully told her family that morning, was a sign of God's love, reminding them of how dark the world would be if there hadn't been that very first Christmas.

Later looking out the cabin window at the falling snow—taking a short break in her grandmother's frenzied Christmas dinner preparations—Marnette wondered if Ina Coulter would still be so cheerful if the Brittons and the Reverend Humphries couldn't make it tomorrow because of all the snow.

She had no doubt about Emilie's reaction, for more than once her cousin had also looked out the window, sighing at the almost knee-high snow that might keep her from sitting across the table from—or maybe even next to—her heart's desire.

Marnette herself would be sorely disappointed, not having seen Drew for a whole week, what with the schoolhouse being closed for the holidays and there being none of those precious head-on-his-shoulder rides home with him in the sleigh. Nor had she been able to trudge through the snow out to their cabin with some lunch for him. Every waking moment of that week had been spent helping Emilie and her grandmother clean up the cabin "for the Lord's birthday"—something Ina Coulter did every year, whether or not they were expecting guests for dinner.

With her wedding gown finished and her Christmas gifts all wrapped (hand-stitched handkerchiefs for everyone in the family and a lovingly monogrammed one for Drew), Marnette really didn't mind all the floor scrubbing, furniture polishing, and curtain washing. She had to admit she would have been happier sprucing up her own cabin for her and Drew's first Christmas together, but he had been stubborn about everything being perfect—the furniture all made, the curtains hung, and their name, "The Brittons," carved above the door—before they crossed the threshold as husband and wife.

Marnette felt a sudden flush at the thought of their wedding night and the bed he had made for them that was bigger than a customary double bed.

She hadn't, at first, understood Emilie's look of dismay when she had seen the big bed the early November Saturday that both of them had driven out to the cabin. But Marnette hadn't known about the patchwork quilt the ladies of the sewing circle had just finished making—not until she'd overheard Grandma telling Emilie that all she and Abbie had to do was add a big enough border of some nice solid color to make the quilt large enough for the extra wide bed..

If Ina Coulter feared her own hand-woven Indian blanket might also be too small, she never did anything about it. Marnette had wondered about all the time her grandmother had been spending out in the barn that fall until she had opened the old woman's cedar chest one day, hoping to find "something old" to add to her wedding gown, and had discovered their second surprise wedding gift.

Still looking out the cabin window, Marnette turned at her grandmother's sudden question from the table where she and Emilie were crimping the edges of tomorrow's mincemeat and pumpkin pies.

"Any sign of them yet?"

"No," Marnette shook her head. She was sure her uncle and the two boys would soon come stomping in from the woods with the family's best Christmas tree ever—something they claimed every year.

Even the scrawniest of trees would be more than Marnette Coulter could ever have hoped for as a child. Back then, Christmas Eve had been just another day to pray her father wouldn't be drunk when he got home.

And though at the boarding school there had been a large ornamented and candled tree in the front parlor, Christmas Eve had been an especially painful time for Marnette as, one by one, all the other girls went off with their parents in carriages or sleighs to spend the holidays at home.

It was during the first of such school-bound Christmases that she and the academy's live-in cook had become such good friends. A childless widow, Katie Sullivan had had no family to go home to, either. And on Christmas Day—having slipped off somewhere the night before for church services—she had cooked a Christmas dinner (using some of her own money, of course) that even Alma Veasley, also having nowhere else to spend the holidays, had begrudgingly admitted was "uncommonly good." The school's spinster headmistress even relinquished a little smile at one of Katie's exaggerated "tales of the ould sod" as the three of them sat eating in the kitchen.

"Sure and didn't we witness another Christmas miracle," Katie said later with a nod upward to the mistress's private room after politely refusing the woman's half-hearted offer to help with the dishes. "Even so," she added, pouring the kettle of hot water into the dish pan, "I wouldn't trust that shifty-eyed Jezebel any more'n I could swallow the blarney stone."

And you were right, Katie, Marnette nodded to herself at the cabin window, thinking of Stuart Whittington's second unanswered letter with its tale of Alma Veasley's lucrative sideline. Once again she marveled that she herself had not been one of the woman's victims.

Could God have had something to do with that? she wondered. Might He have blinded the headmistress to such an easy opportunity for long-distance blackmail?

If Marnette were to believe that, wouldn't she also have to believe that God was a loving Father? And that He did care about her? How else could she explain all the good things that were happening to her? Not the least of those good things was the end of those terrible nightmares. It had been almost six months since she had had the last frightful dream—that night after the children had sung their dreadful song about young Drew at the schoolhouse.

The night of the Founders' Day ball, she had begun having new, happy dreams about herself and Drew Britton. Thinking of some of them made her blush. But she had to smile at the dream from which she had awakened this very morning:

A fire crackled on the old Chappie hearth, and Marnette was bent over a kettle, stirring Drew's favorite stew. Two tiny, yellow-haired babies slept nearby in their lovingly hand-carved, extra wide cradle. When the cabin door opened, she rushed to greet and be swept into the arms of their tall, handsome father.

"Well, it's about time!" said her grandmother as the door of the cabin suddenly burst open and the family's three snow-covered tree cutters stomped in with this year's prize.

"You'd better clean up that mess right now," Ina Coulter said crossly, nodding to the quickly melting snow dripping from their beaver jackets and the branches of the big evergreen.

No one had to ask why she was so cross. They all knew she was angry with herself for always insisting that their tree not be cut until the day before Christmas. Even more, she had not foreseen the morning's light snowfall turning into a full-blown blizzard. They were sure she was thinking of that blizzardy Christmas Eve, two years ago, when Grandpa Newhouse had gone out, alone, to cut a tree and they hadn't found him—in the woods behind the church—until the spring thaw.

It wasn't until the tree was in its stand and strung with popped corn and dried cranberries and they were all seated around the supper table that Ina Coulter admitted it just might be their best ever Christmas tree.

"We had to trudge all the way into the woods behind the old Chappie cabin to find that beauty," said her son, reaching for the bowl of hash.

"Of course," he added with a little wink at Marnette, "we first asked the new owner's permission before we put an axe to her."

He meant Drew, of course, which made Marnette frown. She had thought he would forego any work at the cabin today—he was carving a new mantelpiece for the old fireplace—so he could be home with his family on Christmas Eve.

"Did he say when he would be heading for home?"

Her uncle shook his head. "Only that it probably didn't matter in what cabin he might be snowbound."

"In neither, I hope," said Emilie, for that would mean none of their guests would make it for dinner tomorrow.

"But he did ask me to give you this, Marnie, just in case."

He reached into his shirt pocket and handed her something small in a wrapping of dried cornhusk tied with a bit of string.

Marnette took the small parcel and set it beside her plate. She was sure Drew's sending the gift with her uncle meant he had little hope of seeing her tomorrow. At the same time, she was dying to know what was inside his makeshift wrapping. But that was another of her grandmother's rules: Christmas gifts were never opened until Christmas morning.

But sometimes holiday traditions were broken—especially when everyone else in the family was also dying to know what the town constable had given the schoolmarm the Christmas before they were to be married.

"Open it!" Emilie finally cried in exasperation.

"Before we all die, wondering," nodded her grandmother.

Even Theodore and Robert made faces at the way their cousin hesitated before picking up the little package. The way she so slowly untied the string and just as slowly peeled open the cornhusk wrapping caused more frustration. She sat with a lovesick smile before she gently lifted the tiny carved wooden figure out of its wrapping.

There wasn't a soul in Chappie Creek who would not have recognized the little fairy princess—the tiny bun at the back of her head, her nose so high in the air, and the three books so jealously clasped to her breast—that Drew Britton had begun carving for the children one Indian summer day.

"And what are you going to do with that?" said Theodore. A logical question, since Christmas gifts were always something a body needed: new stockings or mittens and at least one new handkerchief. His brother and his father—and maybe even his grandmother—might have asked the same thing.

But his sister Emilie would never have asked such a question. Though she knew as well as Marnette that it meant neither of them would see their loves on Christmas Day, she wistfully smiled at the tender kiss Marnette gave the little hand-carved doll before she set it up on the fireplace mantel between their grandmother's prized pewter plates.

&

It took three days for the Coulters to dig out from Chappie Creek's Christmas blizzard of 1848. On the fourth day, when Thad Coulter thought he was going to get a rest, his mother nagged him into harnessing the mare to their small cutter for a sleigh ride into the trading post to pick up a few items she had run short of while she had been so busy with her Christmas cleaning. He might have put off the trip one more day if one of those items had not been baking powder. His sons weren't the only ones who had begun making faces at Grandma's leathery flapjacks and nuggety biscuits.

He also gave in to Marnette when she begged to go along, since they would pass the old Chappie cabin and he knew she was anxious to check on Drew—in case he had been snow-bound there.

If he had, Marnette could only wonder what, or if, he had been eating. She stopped worrying when they saw sledge tracks leading to and from the cabin. But she was disappointed when she read the brief note that was tacked to the door.

> Marnie—
>   Gone with my Pa to the village. Hope to be
> back by New Year's Eve.
>   —Drew

He meant the Indian village, of course, and their using the big sledge no doubt meant he and his father had gone out there with not only a supply of medicine, but a load of food as well.

"Now that," said her uncle, "is what it means to be a Christian."

He did not say what they were both thinking: Some folks in town wouldn't care if all the Indians starved. Marnette herself couldn't deny a pinch of resentment at the fact that some Indian woman might smile at—or even touch—Drew Britton when she hadn't set eyes on him in almost two weeks. It was possible that he and his father might not make it back by New Year's Eve, especially if there were some sick Indian children who needed tending.

She was sure Emilie, who was also looking forward to see-ing—and hopefully dancing with—one of the Brittons at the first New Year's Eve ball in their new town hall, would be equally downcast.

With the cutter again headed for the trading post, Marnette looked back at the cabin that was soon to be her home. Even with the two new rooms, the curtains in the windows, and their name above the door, it looked empty and abandoned with no trail of smoke from the chimney.

"I think maybe we ought to double up on some of those items on Grandma's list," her uncle said, pulling the bearskin lap robe up over their knees. "She's probably right about the year ending in a deep freeze."

Marnette's sudden shiver was her only reply. She was wondering just how warm an Indian tepee might be for a visiting doctor and his son.

Though she herself got thoroughly warmed up from the stove at the trading post, by the time they got home, Marnette was shivering again, mostly with an icy fear.

When she got into bed that night, no amount of covers or even Emilie's warm body beside her was enough to take away the chill. The longer she lay shivering in the dark with Drew's note tightly clutched in her hand, the stronger became her fear that their being kept apart at Christmas—and most likely New Year's Day, too—was a bad omen.

But wasn't that her own fault for allowing herself to be so happy these past four months?

What right had she, conceived in sin, to expect any amount of happiness in this world or the next—especially when she had committed so many sins of her own? She trembled all the more at remembering the many lies to her prairie family and how she never told the man she was to marry the truth about her past.

"What's wrong?" Emilie finally asked her.

Marnette would have said "nothing," except for her vow not to tell any more lies. "I'm afraid."

"Of what?"

"That something bad is going to happen."

Emilie turned on her side. "Probably a touch of cabin fever. I'm getting kind of edgy, too, being cooped up inside so long."

"No, this is real. I can feel it in my bones."

"Then maybe you should pray."

"Yes," Marnette nodded. "Maybe I should pray."

But Marnette Coulter had never prayed in her life. How could she pray, now, when she was sure God Himself was going to make something bad happen to punish her for daring to be so happy. Something that would keep her from walking up the aisle to become Drew Britton's wife on the fifteenth day of January, 1849.

eighteen

Ina Coulter had been right about the deep freeze. And maybe Emilie had been right, too, about Marnette's merely having a touch of cabin fever. For on New Year's Eve, as she was dressing for the ball that night, Marnette's thoughts were anything but morbid or fearful.

Learning that Drew and his father had safely made it back from the Indian village played no small part in the lift of her spirits. Nothing could dampen those spirits now, not even the fact that Drew would not be coming to escort her to the ball.

"I told him not to bother," her uncle said, recounting his having met the doctor's homebound sledge on the road. "That we'd all be coming tonight in the big sleigh."

That her grandmother and the two boys were also going to the ball was a last-minute surprise, too. It probably meant that they, too, were tired of being cooped up in the cabin, first by the snow and then by the lingering sub-zero freeze.

It had been almost three weeks since she had seen Drew, and Marnette's spirits were the highest as she slipped into her best winter gown of lace-trimmed sky blue delaine, not the least bit disturbed that this winter the shirred pearl-buttoned bodice was somewhat tighter. She smiled at the way the skirt—yards and yards of the soft wool and cotton fabric—billowed out when she twirled before the mirror.

There would be no matronly schoolmarm's bun tonight, she suddenly decided. She was a young woman, dressing for the man she loved. With that, she pulled out all her hairpins to let her dark mane cascade down to her shoulders. She caught up only the sides in a pearl-studded comb at the back of her head and then stole two small wisps out of the comb to form a seductive ringlet before each of her ears.

Though she was more than satisfied with her hair, Marnette frowned at her face in the mirror. Dusky though her complexion might be, her cheeks had long since lost their summertime bloom. But didn't she, like her cousin, know a remedy for that? *Yes*. And she knew exactly where Emilie hid her little tole painted rouge pot: in her draw-stringed reticule hanging from one of the bedposts.

If ever their grandmother might discover it, Emilie had a ready argument for using the rouge: If it were not dishonest for a Chappie Creek housewife to add carrot dye to the freshly-churned butter to make it more appealing, why was it any more dishonest for a girl to add some color to her cheeks for the same reason?

After smoothing just a hint of pink onto each of her cheeks, Marnette fondly smiled toward the other room where Emilie was before the fire, pressing the pink paisley gown that she would wear—along with her own store-bought rosy cheeks—to the ball.

It occurred to Marnette that today she had smiled more than she had in her entire life. To think that God would punish her for that could not be right.

Later, huddled between Grandma and Emilie in the big family sleigh with her heart pounding at the thought of seeing Drew, Marnette was sure there was nothing in the world that could spoil this happiest of New Year's Eves.

❧

"Oh, isn't it lovely?" Emilie cried after they walked into the decorated hall.

"Yes, it is nice," her grandmother nodded, a surprising admission from one who had little room for gewgaws or gimcracks in her life. The only decorations in the Coulter cabin were sheaves of drying herbs or strings of hardening berries hung from the rafters during the winter and, of course, the popped-corn-and-berry strung Christmas tree.

Even Theodore and Robert seemed somewhat awed at how the ladies of the New Year's Eve decorating committee had turned the new town hall into a festooned fairyland.

Feathery garlands of fragrant, bow-tied evergreens seemed to be draped everywhere: over each window and doorway and trimming not only the councilmen's platform, but the cloth-covered sweets table as well. Here and there were sprigs of imported holly and clusters of mistletoe from the nearby woods—both probably having been wrapped in straw and burlap sometime in the fall and kept fresh for the holidays in somebody's spring house. The biggest cluster of mistletoe hung just above the door of the cloakroom, which was where the family now headed to hang up their heavy winter wraps.

But Marnette Coulter was interested in only one particular town hall decoration, and she didn't smile until, lingering in the cloakroom doorway, she saw his handsome blond head towering over the others in a small circle of young men talking near the council platform where Tim Piper would, no doubt, soon be playing his fiddle.

She stood in the doorway, waiting for Drew to notice her. She wasn't about to step onto any dance floor, unescorted, even though every one of the young men at the town hall that night knew Marnette Coulter was anything but fair game.

Finally Drew turned his head toward the cloakroom. When he came purposefully striding toward her, Marnette glanced overhead at the big cluster of bow-tied mistletoe and inched backward, into the room. He wouldn't need any mistletoe over her head, and she wanted their first New Year's Eve kiss to be private.

She had not been aware that someone else had also lingered in the farthest and darkest corner of the cloakroom—someone who had already received a number of kisses.

But the town constable had somehow found out. When he stormed into the cloakroom, he gave Marnette a shove that would have slammed her against the wall except for all those bulky winter wraps.

Only as a child had Marnette seen such fury in a man's face. Drew's teeth clenched and his nostrils flared like a charging bull's.

"I've caught you this time, Piper!"

Like an explosion, two bodies suddenly flew out of the cloakroom. First, Tim Piper, as if he had been struck by a bolt of lightning. Then Drew Britton, lunging for his throat.

"I'll kill you!"

And then the two of them were down on the floor: the town clerk, gasping for air, and the town constable on top of him, pounding his head on the floor like a sledgehammer.

Marnette closed her eyes and covered her ears. But that didn't help—any more than it had helped when she had been a child. Suddenly she was again a terrified little girl, cringing behind her bedroom door at the sickening sound of her burly six-foot father beating her frail five-foot mother. The sum and substance of all her nightmarish dreams.

Why didn't her mother scream? Why—when she surely knew what was coming—did she merely stand there like some mindless mute, waiting for all those blows?

One! The wide, sweeping slap that always sent her thudding against the kitchen wall.

Two! The backhanded whack on the other cheek that slammed her head into the wall.

Three! The one that always sent Marenette tearing to her room.

Four! Five! Six! After that, she would lose count. But it never ended until she heard her mother fall into a heap on the floor where she would lie in wait for the final blow: that furious and deadly kick.

"No, Papa! No!"

Again Marnette felt something akin to a shove, this time by Wilting Sunflower—tearing out of the cloakroom, screaming for her brother to *"Stop!"*

But he didn't.

Not until Doc Britton pushed through the growing ring of onlookers to perform a bit of emergency surgery: pulling his totally crazed son off the blue-faced town clerk.

By then Marnette had buried her face in the nearest of heavy coats and she neither saw nor heard what happened next: Wilting Sunflower, cradled Tim's head on her lap as her father listened—first to Tim Piper's heart and then to what his half-Indian daughter was tearfully telling him.

Doc Britton angrily looked up at his still half-crazy son. "You know what you did? Almost killed your future brother-in-law!"

᠄ᴥ

It was some time before the circle of onlookers broke up, and a good while longer before there was any music for their first New Year's Eve ball.

They would talk about it—some of them even joke about it —for months to come: that the first peace-disturbing culprit in their town constable's short career had been none other than Drew Britton himself.

But most of them didn't think he should have resigned. And none of them would ever understand why Marnette Coulter had—only two weeks before they were to be married—broken their engagement.

But none of them knew anything about her past. Drew himself didn't know. Nor did he have any idea what was going on in her mind when he finally found her that night in the cloakroom, fiercely getting back into her coat.

She had been blind, but now she could see. She would not

make the same mistake her mother had made by marrying a man she knew was capable of murder. One murder she had only heard about, but one she had almost witnessed tonight.

"Marnie! I've been looking all over for you!"

When he reached for her, she pulled away. "Don't touch me, Drew!"

He stared at her in disbelief. *Don't touch me?* From the woman he had so steadfastly courted and for whom he had been working so hard? His partner in all those passionate kisses?

When he tried to take her in his arms and kiss her, she again pulled away.

"Marnie—I love you!"

"Don't say that! I don't want to hear it!"

"With all my heart!"

"Heart?" she almost screamed.

She saw his face again, the look on it when he had earlier shoved her against the wall. It had looked just like her father's face, every time he had gone after her mother.

"You don't *have* a heart! You're nothing but a cold-blooded killer!"

nineteen

Homer Farnsworth checked the calendar on the wall behind his counter, just to make sure. He agreed with all those old cronies sitting around the stove that it had been the longest and coldest winter they could remember and the slowest-arriving spring.

Finally the late April sun had coaxed small avalanches of snow off the town's rooftops, and little rivers of melted ice had begun glistening in the wagon ruts on the road. Yesterday Homer had seen some violets on his way to the outhouse.

But an even surer sign of spring would be the arrival of the first stagecoach, due in one more day. The appearance of the eastern stagecoach was a welcome event for most Chappie Creek families because in the big mail pouch would be long-awaited letters from relatives back East, as well as the goods some of the folks had ordered last fall.

The Newhouses probably would have been among the most eager for such a delivery—Grandma Newhouse had finally ordered some eyeglasses—except that the stubborn little matriarch had died of pneumonia back in February. It seemed like yesterday because the ground had been frozen solid back then and the family had had to keep her body in the spring house until a few weeks ago. A tale to be told around the trading post stove for many a winter to come was that Rheba Newhouse had been kept on ice, much like her husband, Royal, before she had finally been laid to rest.

Some of the families with young children would be tickled to see the stagecoach come in, knowing that when it went out again, Leah Jaster and her four troublesome children would be on it. Having finally sold her farm in bits and pieces to neighboring families, the widow said she was going east to take her delicate female condition to a more civilized doctor. Everyone knew the condition she was really seeking a cure for was her widowhood.

Homer doubted, though, if anyone knew why Marnette Coulter would also be on that coach when it headed back. But he wasn't going to wear any black armband—he had always thought Ina Coulter's uppity Boston granddaughter had never belonged in Chappie Creek. And he was sure all those families who had been bamboozled into letting their girls go to school would be relieved to know that Ina's other granddaughter—a prairie-born girl who knew a woman's place in life—had agreed to fill in at the schoolhouse until the board found somebody else.

That wasn't the only job that was open in Chappie Creek. The town council was still bickering over who they should appoint as town constable—and maybe town clerk, too, unless Tim Piper came back from wherever it was that he and Wilting Sunflower had run off to and gotten married two weeks ago. Done both themselves and the town a big favor; a wedding like that would be more like a wake.

Too bad Drew Britton couldn't see the favor Marnette Coulter had done for him in breaking their engagement. A body didn't have enough fingers to count the girls in town who would jump at the chance to spend the rest of their lives cooking and cleaning for the doctor's only son, whether or not he could support a wife just mending broken furniture and carving tombstones.

But he would probably have to shave off that beard—and most certainly take a bath—before he started any serious courting. Homer had barely recognized him when he'd come into the post a couple weeks ago and bought the few remaining cans of food on the shelf: like some half crazy hermit, holding his own private wake out there at the old Chappie cabin.

And what would he do the day after tomorrow when she got on that stagecoach for Boston? Shoot himself?

ɞ

As her uncle tied the mare to the hitching post, Marnette watched her grandmother walk up the steps of the trading post to take care of the first of her errands that had brought her, by buckboard, into town: bringing her hand-woven Indian blanket for Homer Farnsworth to carefully wrap and add to all the luggage that would be securely strapped, under a canvas, atop the outgoing stagecoach tomorrow. She had insisted Marnette take the blanket, for she knew winters could be cold in Boston, too, especially for an unmarried governess sleeping alone—no matter how civilized her city accommodations might be.

Turning away to embark on her own morning errand, Marnette asked herself if she would actually be able to get on that stagecoach and leave all of them behind, especially Grandma, knowing she most likely would never see any of them again.

But she simply had to. She no longer could live in the same town with Drew Britton, knowing how close she had come to doing the same thing her mother had: marry a man who was guilty of murder.

The past four months had been pure agony, especially passing the old Chappie cabin every time her uncle had taken her to and from the schoolhouse. This morning would give her more agony. For, though Drew hadn't shown up at church for all those months, she wasn't sure he didn't sometimes come back to his family's cabin.

But she knew her grandmother was right. Though she had already said goodbye to her students, Marnette should make a farewell visit to all those families who had in one way or another touched her life in Chappie Creek.

Drawing a deep breath, Marnette put her reluctant feet onto the puddled road and headed for the first cabin on her list: that of Douglas and Lorna Howlett. With still-nightgowned children scrambling about and Lorna's new baby bawling for its breakfast, Marnette's murmured goodbye was almost lost in the din.

From the Howletts' she walked to the Cunninghams', and from there to the Pipers'. Though Angus Piper merely nodded gruffly, his wife, Mattie, said something about being sorry to see the town's most able and amiable seamstress leave. Marnette was embarrassed by the last-minute compliment, but she was not sorry when Mattie said nothing about the two wedding gowns: the one Wilting Sunflower had never asked her to make (what color would she have chosen?) and Marnette's own never-worn gown of white satin, tucked away—hopefully someday for Emilie—in their grandmother's cedar chest.

From the Pipers' she walked to the Fairfields' and from there to the small, crowded cabin of the Newhouses, still with its black-ribboned wreath on the door. That would be her grandmother's second errand that morning: trudging up to Massacre Hill to pay her respects at its newest of graves.

Her next farewell call would have been at the parsonage, but the white scarf tied to the hitching post told her the Reverend Richard Humphries was not there.

The very last stop in Marnette's round of farewells was the one she knew would cause her the most pain. But she couldn't leave tomorrow without having said goodbye to Doc Britton, the one who had brought her home to Chappie Creek almost four years ago.

As she approached the doctor's cabin, Marnette's heart suddenly sank. Coming out of the cabin—his step so quick and his head so erect she at first thought it was Drew—was the Reverend Humphries. He met her at the gate, and even then she might not have recognized him except for his white turned-around collar, for never had she seen the pastor's eyes so bright or his mouth so wide in a smile. Marnette could actually see his struggle to come down out of the clouds when she tendered her roadside farewell.

"I hope you've given this move a good deal of thought, Marnette."

"I have, Reverend—for months." Four long, agonizing months, waiting for the trail to open.

Since there had been no way of getting any letter to him, Stuart Whittington had no idea Marnette was finally taking him up on his offer to come live with him and his growing family—and the world's most irreverent but lovable cook.

Well, her arrival in Chappie Creek had been a surprise. It was not so strange that her arrival in Boston should also be a surprise.

"You'll never find God by running away, Marnette," said the pastor.

God? Whatever made him think she was looking for God?

"Everyone hungers for God's love," he told her, "though some of us don't even know it. And most of us look in the wrong places. All we have to do is look into our own hearts."

Marnette turned away, fearful the reverend might do just that: look into her eyes and finally see the scarlet letter on her soul. If he did, would he still talk about a loving and merciful God? Or would he have to admit it was an offended and angry God who had punished the daughter of Thomas and Cynthia Coulter for being born.

The sin of the mother had, indeed, been visited upon the child. Why else had Marnette's first—and only—love been a man with another man's blood on his hands?

But it was all going to end with her. Marnette Coulter would never marry any man, and the sin would never be visited upon anyone else. Besides, as governess to Stuart Whittington's adopted girls, she would have more than enough "daughters" to take care of—maybe even love.

"Of course, if things don't work out in Boston," said the

pastor, "you can always come back."

"That's true."

But Marnette knew she would never come back. And again she turned away, this time so the reverend would not see her struggle to fight back the tears that had been threatening ever since she had begun her round of farewells.

"But I'm sorry you're going to miss the wedding," said the reverend.

"Wedding?"

"Yes." And Marnette turned back in time to see his smiling ascent back up into the clouds. "I finally got the courage to ask her—and Abigail said yes."

Of course!

Hadn't Abbie Britton been one of the most faithful students at his weekly Bible study? And hadn't they been together since August on all those Gospel-spreading trips out to the Indian village? And all these years of helping her father, caring for other people's chest colds and chilblains, wasn't it as if the doctor's daughter had been practicing for an even more important role (now caring for their souls) as the pastor's second wife?

Those thoughts were suddenly followed by another: Once Doc Britton's second daughter was married, he would be living all alone. Unless Drew decided to sell the old Chappie cabin and come back home. . .

"I'm happy," Marnette managed to smile at the pastor. "For both of you."

"And you can tell that to Abigail over a hot cup of tea," he smiled back. "She's had the kettle on and been waiting for you since you first started out on your rounds."

Marnette glanced toward the cabin, fervently hoping Abbie Britton's twin brother wasn't also waiting.

But if she had expected to be greeted at the door by a starry-eyed and blushing bride-to-be, Marnette was disappointed. Though Abbie smilingly accepted her congratulations, it was a somewhat sad little smile.

"I hope you can stay for some tea," she said, nodding to the table near the fireplace, with its waiting pot of tea and platter of freshly-baked sweet rolls.

"Of course," Marnette nodded. But she didn't want to stay too long in the cabin where Drew Britton had so long lived.

"I'm sorry my father isn't home," Abbie said, pouring their first steaming cup of tea. "He was called out during the night to that new family, the Vadens. Her first baby—and that sometimes takes a while. But I'm sure he'll stop off at your uncle's on his way back. I know he won't let you leave without saying goodbye."

"I hope not."

Throughout their customary feminine tea talk, the doctor's daughter seemed preoccupied with some inner sadness. Marnette herself couldn't help thinking how, if things had been different, she and Abbie Britton might have been family.

No. She had promised not to torture herself with thoughts like that.

But as she got up from the table to leave, Marnette noticed a dozen or so hand-carved figurines neatly arranged on the Brittons' fireplace mantel. As if knowing who had done the carving was not enough torture, she took one of the wooden figures down for an even closer look.

She at once recognized the kneeling figure as Wilting Sunflower, her head slightly bent—as if in prayer. As she gently turned the figure over in her hands, Marnette also knew it was more than just an idle man's whittling. The grace of the pose and each feature so delicately carved in the tiny face—this was poetry, too. No, it was even more than that: It was a labor of love.

A man would have to love a girl deeply to carve a figure like that. Enough to want to knock another man senseless if he thought that man was taking advantage of her. Enough to kill yet another man who had taken the most ravaging advantage.

No! She couldn't let herself think something like that. For then she would have to ask herself if she wasn't wrong—hadn't always been wrong—about Drew Britton.

"These are only a few of my brother's carvings," Abbie said, coming to the fireplace. "Most of them he's given away."

"Yes, I know," Marnette nodded. And suddenly there was a large unswallowable lump in her throat. She was thinking of the little wooden fairy princess—his Christmas gift—which she had, only a week later, thrown into the fire.

"I wish he hadn't," said his sister, "because I'm afraid he'll never do anymore." Marnette saw tears suddenly brimming Abbie's eyes. "That he might be out there at the old cabin—carving his own tombstone."

Marnette gave her an uncomprehending—yet suddenly frightened—look through her own blur of tears.

"Never coming into town, never answering the door. We don't know what—or even if—he's been eating."

Marnette stared at Abbie Britton. Surely she wasn't talking about her always so vibrant and cocky twin brother.

"You're the only girl he ever loved, Marnette," Abbie said quietly. "Loved you from the day he first set eyes on you."

It was like a knife thrust into her breast. And his sister apparently saw Marnette flinch at the thrust because she lay an apologetic hand on her arm.

"I'm not saying it's your fault, Marnette. I'm sure he would have gotten over you in time. It's that other thing he can't live with—always had trouble living with."

Other thing?

"Hated all those old-timers' stories around the stove and the way the younger boys always gawked at him. Died a little bit, too, every time he heard that terrible song."

Marnette flinched again. The "other thing" was that fatal

day in the woods—the killing that had always stood between her and Drew Britton.

"But he was able to live with it," Abbie said with more tears brimming her eyes. "Until that terrible day only a few weeks ago. With our sister."

Marnette stared dumbly. What was Abbie saying: that Wilting Sunflower was not able to forgive Drew for almost killing the man she loved? And that was why she and Tim Piper had eloped?

"It wasn't true," said Abbie. "But for Drew's sake, she let him and everyone else in town go on believing it all these years."

"Believing what?" Marnette feebly asked.

"That Otis Grimes had raped her."

Marnette was beyond being shocked at Abbie Britton's actually saying the word that no one—in all their whisperings behind Wilting Sunflower's back—had ever spoken.

"She knew it would kill him to know the truth."

"The truth?"

"That Otis had only been trying to help her when Drew shot him—trying to pry open the bear trap she hadn't seen in the dark."

Oh, no! It was almost a prayer. But Marnette still was not able to pray—not even to ask God's mercy for someone else. How could any man live with the knowledge that he had killed someone by mistake?

"But why?" she whispered. "After all these years—why did she decide to tell him now?"

"She didn't," said Abbie. "It just happened the day he went up to Massacre Hill to set Grandma Newhouse's gravestone. He found Wilting Sunflower laying flowers on Otis' grave."

"Violets," Marnette whispered again.

"Yes," Abbie nodded. "I wondered every spring about that, too." She drew a deep and quivery breath. "Anyway, that's when she blurted it out. And that's why she talked Tim into eloping—so she could walk up the aisle somewhere else wearing white. Then she could give Tim the gift of knowing she was coming to his bed a virgin and still not hurt Drew by letting anyone else in town know the terrible truth."

Cradling the carved figure of Wilting Sunflower in her hand, Marnette thought, *Now that is true love—to have been so cruelly maligned for so many years and be concerned only with sparing her brother more pain. How did a person learn to love like that?*

"She's always had a deep prayer life," said Abbie, taking the little kneeling figure from Marnette to gently caress it before setting it back on the mantel. "Sometimes getting up, even before dawn, to slip out to the woods to pray."

That was not strange to Marnette—her grandmother often did the same thing. Perhaps it was the Indian way.

"And that's how she happened to be out in the woods that morning when Drew set out for some early hunting."

Abbie looked toward the woods as if able to see the tragic happening that had given both her sister and brother so many years of torment.

"My father has always known how much it haunted Drew. That's why he's so worried about him now. Afraid it might be like it was with my mother."

Once again Marnette got that frightened feeling, more so because now she understood what Abbie had said earlier about Drew "carving his own tombstone."

"It wasn't guilt that killed my mother, Marnette. It was despair. She didn't believe God could forgive her for causing that old Indian woman's death."

"But that was an accident," said Marnette. "An accident with Drew, too."

"Yes," Abbie nodded. "But there's no way to convince him of that—not when he won't even open the door."

She searched Marnette's face, as if for some ray of hope. But

Marnette quickly looked away so Drew Britton's sister wouldn't see what she feared was clearly in her eyes: her own guilt.

"I'd better go now," she said, nodding toward the door. "My uncle and grandmother are waiting for me at the post."

Abbie merely nodded. But at the door, she placed her hand on Marnette's arm. "I don't know why you're going back to Boston, Marnette, but I can't believe it's because you don't love my brother."

She apparently took Marnette's silence as assent.

"And I can't believe, either, that he wouldn't open the door for you."

Again Marnette turned away. She knew Abbie was asking that her last stop be at the old Chappie cabin, that she say something to Drew that might keep him from sinking into a pit of despair.

"I can't."

"Why?"

"Because it *is* my fault."

When Marnette passed the town hall on her way to the trading post, her own condemnation was still ringing in her ears: *You're nothing but a cold-blooded killer!*

twenty

When she got to the trading post, Marnette was surprised to find only her uncle waiting on the wooden bench beside the door.

"Your grandma's waiting for you up on the hill," he told her somewhat gruffly. "She was sure you wouldn't want to leave without saying goodbye to some of the folks there, too."

She thought she saw a fleeting look of sadness on his face: the first and only hint that he might be sorry to see her go. And she wondered if tomorrow she would dare hug this bearded brother of Thomas Coulter who was so kind and yet so shy in his affections.

"She's right," Marnette nodded with a glance toward Massacre Hill. Though she had promised herself last summer never to go back to the town's place of the dead, Marnette knew she could not leave Chappie Creek without saying goodbye to Sarah Humphries.

The sky had turned a dismal gray, as if to match the grim gravestones on Massacre Hill. Even the big pine wreath from Founders' Day had the look of death: most of its brown needles fallen onto the ground and its weather-beaten purple bow sadly drooping down. Marnette was sure the bouquet of violets on the other side of the hill would be withered, too.

No. She was not going to think of that. She would quickly say goodbye to Sarah Humphries and end the morning's grief.

But it wasn't possible for her to pass even the first two gravestones at the bottom of the hill without thinking of the couple who lay, side by side, beneath them: Leo and Lorna Chappie. What would they think of the bustling town that bore their name? What would they think of all those changes in their tiny log cabin?

No! She wouldn't think of that, either.

Passing all those other stones was safer—those with barely readable names that meant nothing to Marnette Coulter because she had no faces nor any little stories to go with them. What had happened to all those men, women, and children on the terrible day that had given the hill its name was a tragic story, but it had nothing to do with her.

No, that wasn't true. If the Chappie Creek massacre had never happened, there never would have been that other killing in the woods. And her own story would not have such an unhappy ending.

She let out a deep sigh, for there was not a stone on Massacre Hill that would not cause her some pain. But she didn't have to go looking for it, she told herself, turning to find the only grave she had come to visit.

She always had trouble finding Sarah Humphries' grave—probably because she thought Sarah should have been buried in her beloved Hartford. But surely the pastor's saintly young wife was happy now. And if she was able to look down, wouldn't she be happier to know her husband would not have to spend the rest of his life alone?

What would her cousin Emilie be hoping, once Abbie Britton got married and moved into the parsonage? Would Doc Britton—no longer with any woman to take care of him—now consider taking another wife?

I hope so, Emilie, Marnette thought with a sad little smile. Sad, because she knew she would not be around to find out. Once she got on the stagecoach, she would never again see her cousin who might have been more like a sister, if only Marnette had not had so many secrets of her own.

She still had not found Sarah's grave when she came upon a warped wooden marker with its crudely carved name blurred by both time and weather: Jessica Hawley Britton. Beside it stood the nameless wooden cross that marked the grave of her baby who had been born dead.

It wasn't guilt that killed my mother...it was despair.

No! She must not think of that! Because then she would have to think of what else Abbie Britton had said about her brother.

Like it was with my mother...out there at the old cabin, carving his own tombstone.

Marnette couldn't resist looking in the direction of the old Chappie cabin. But still she could not pray—not even to ask God to send someone to the cabin who would say the right thing to keep Drew Britton from dying, like his mother, of despair. How could she pray when she knew that she herself had delivered the fatal blow?

When she again looked down again at his mother's grave, it was with something sorely akin to despair. She might have gone down on her knees if she hadn't suddenly turned at the sound of her grandmother's voice behind her.

"Maybe someday," said Ina Coulter, "our stonecutter will carve a new one for his mother."

Marnette said nothing. She was more concerned about another new tombstone and what it might say.

"A son should always honor his mother's grave," said her grandmother. "A daughter should, too—if only in her heart."

As she stared at her grandmother, Marnette's heart skipped a beat. Was she saying that she knew Marnette had never seen her own mother's grave?

And did she know why?

"No matter how her mother had died," said Ina Coulter. "Or lived before she died."

Marnette continued to stare at the half-Indian woman who might also have been something more than a grandmother if Marnette had not so fearfully kept her heart under lock and key the past four years.

"What are you telling me, Grandma?"

"What I should have told you a long time ago. I know what you've been trying to hide all these years—the truth about your mother."

Marnette looked for some place to sit down. But there was no resting place for the living on Massacre Hill.

"How?" She needed to know how her grandmother had learned the terrible truth.

"It doesn't matter how," said Ina Coulter, still convinced she had done the right thing in burning that evil blackmail letter. "What matters is what you've been carrying in your heart all these years."

Marnette turned away from the soul-piercing look in her grandmother's dark eyes.

"That's why you never went to Bible study and had to be dragged to church every Sunday. Because you were afraid you might hear that story again."

Marnette turned back. "What story?"

"About Jesus and the woman caught in adultery. Because if you ever came to believe it—that God could forgive a woman like that—then you would have to lay down your own stones. The stones you've been hurling in your heart at your mother all these years."

Marnette stared at her grandmother. How could she know all this if not with the help of some unearthly power?

"Trying to be holier than God," her grandmother went on. "Denying your mother His forgiveness, because then you would have to do the same. You even tried to punish the Lord for that—by making Him into some kind of merciless monster."

"But you don't know the whole ugly truth, Grandma." Marnette nodded toward the wooden cross that marked the grave of Jessica Britton's stillborn baby. "I'm the one who never should have been born."

"Because you were on the way before wedlock?"

Again Marnette looked for and failed to find some place to sit down. She had no way of knowing that this time her grandmother was merely guessing.

But if she thought Ina Coulter would admit that they were talking about an unforgivable sin, she was due for another knee-buckling surprise.

"There's never been a person born—or stillborn—that God didn't already love in the womb. And that's probably another of the Holy Scriptures that you never wanted to hear."

But Marnette heard it now. God speaking so long ago through his prophet, Jeremiah, and only last Sunday through his faithful minister at the Chappie Creek church: *Before I formed thee in the womb I knew thee.*

"It isn't God who's been punishing you, Marnette. You've been punishing yourself in an attempt to punish your mother for being only human."

Marnette tried to deny it, but she couldn't.

"Don't you suppose she did a good enough job punishing herself?"

Once again Marnette felt a strangling lump in her throat. Was that why her mother never screamed, why she mutely stood there, taking all those blows? To punish herself for her sin?

But if Cynthia Coulter was so concerned about sin, how could she have then become a woman of the street? Or was that self-inflicted punishment, too? Had Marnette's mother believed the curse her own mother had called down upon them on the steps of the Boston church that terrible Sunday when Marnette had been only ten?

"I don't know who put all this bilge about God in your head, Marnette," her grandmother said almost angrily. "But it was all a lie. There is no sin that God won't forgive—if only we ask Him."

Marnette stood in silence, thinking. Who could be sure her

mother hadn't asked God's forgiveness before she'd died? And what right had she to assume that anyone might be burning in hell?

Suddenly the lump in her throat dissolved in a surge of tears.

And because Marnette Coulter could not do it on the grave of her own mother, she did it on the grave of someone else's. She sank down on her knees and silently wept into her hands.

I love you, Mama—I've always loved you!

twenty-one

For months Ina Coulter had been praying for some little miracle—something that would keep Marnette from getting on that stagecoach. And as she came down from Massacre Hill in a flurry of snowflakes, she wondered if this wasn't it.

No, there had never been an April snow that hadn't quickly melted.

And how many favors could she hope for in a single day? Hadn't it been a gift from God that Marnette had finally been able to forgive her mother?

Besides, it was selfish for Ina to want the girl to stay. Especially when she knew that, except for those few months of betrothal, Marnette had never been happy in Chappie Creek.

❧

Marnette could only wonder how long she had been kneeling at Jessica Britton's grave. For when she finally looked up, her grandmother was gone and she herself was covered with snow.

April snow—a sign of God's love?

If so, it was not the only sign the Lord had given on Massacre Hill that spring morning. For when she got to her feet, Marnette felt as if the weight of the world had been lifted from her soul. She knew that only a loving and merciful God could have done that.

When she raised her snow-lashed eyes to heaven, not a single word would come. How did you talk to God when you had never talked to Him before? How did you thank Him for such a wonderful gift?

Hopefully, she would be able to thank Him tonight, kneeling at her bed. Or maybe she would have to do it like her grandmother—out in the woods. And maybe, if she prayed hard enough and long enough, she would someday also be able to forgive her father. And her other grandmother, too.

But how many prayers would it take for her to be able to forgive herself for the monstrous lie she had carved into Drew Britton's soul on New Year's Eve?

Suddenly it didn't matter if she could ever forgive herself. Or even that Drew might never forgive her. What mattered was that he knew it was a lie!

With that, Marnette turned and began quickly walking—and then running—down Massacre Hill. Hopefully she would find her grandmother and uncle waiting in the loaded buckboard, ready for the ride back home that would take them past the old Chappie cabin.

Suddenly a prayer came from the depths of her heart. Only later would she wonder if God minded that her very first prayer was for somebody else. *Please, God,* she prayed. *Please make him open the door. Please, Lord—make him listen to me!*

ಶ

Only when she was halfway down the hill did Marnette realize she was on the wrong side—the side where only Otis Grimes had been buried.

But it was finding someone kneeling at that grave that made her stop dead in her tracks. Because of all the snow, but mostly because of the beard, she thought it was Doc Britton. Only when he stood up, did she know it was his son. *Drew!*

He didn't turn to see who was coming down the hill in such a rush, even when she was standing, breathless, beside him. He merely bent down to brush some snow from the new gravestone, so she could clearly see what the freshly-carved letters said. The words chilled her soul:

OTIS GRIMES
Killed in Cold Blood
by Andrew John Britton

"Now everyone will know the truth," he said, still not looking at her.

"But it's not true," she insisted. "And what I told you—that was a lie, too."

He turned and looked at her—misery covered his face. "He was only trying to help her, and I killed him!"

"Only to save her, Drew. Only because you loved her."

She thought she also saw a glint of hope in his green eyes. Until he shook his head.

"God will never forgive what I did, Marnie—never."

"He already has, Drew. And now you must forgive yourself."

"I can't."

"Then I'll help you, sweetheart."

Now she did see hope in his eyes. For, if she were to help him, wouldn't she have to stay in town?

Yes. And to make that perfectly clear, Marnette slipped her arms around him. "I love you, Drew. I'll always love you."

It took some time for her words to sink in. Only then did she feel his arms around her. "Don't leave me, Marnie—ever!"

"Never," she told him. And that was the truth.

A Letter To Our Readers

Dear Reader:

In order that we might better contribute to your reading enjoyment, we would appreciate your taking a few minutes to respond to the following questions. When completed, please return to the following:

Rebecca Germany, Editor
Heartsong Presents
P.O. Box 719
Uhrichsville, Ohio 44683

1. Did you enjoy reading *His Name on her Heart*?
   ❑ Very much. I would like to see more books
      by this author!
   ❑ Moderately
      I would have enjoyed it more if _____

   _____

2. Are you a member of *Heartsong Presents*? Yes   No
   If no, where did you purchase this book? _____

   _____

3. What influenced your decision to purchase this
   book? (Check those that apply.)

   ❑ Cover   ❑ Back cover copy

   ❑ Title   ❑ Friends

   ❑ Publicity   ❑ Other _____

4. On a scale from 1 (poor) to 10 (superior), please rate the following elements.

___Heroine   ___Plot

___Hero   ___Inspirational theme

___Setting   ___Secondary characters

5. What settings would you like to see covered in *Heartsong Presents* books?

_____

_____

6. What are some inspirational themes you would like to see treated in future books?_____

_____

_____

7. Would you be interested in reading other *Heartsong Presents* titles?   ❏ Yes   ❏ No

8. Please check your age range:
❏ Under 18   ❏ 18-24   ❏ 25-34
❏ 35-45   ❏ 46-55   ❏ Over 55

9. How many hours per week do you read? —————

Name _____

Occupation _____

Address _____

City _____ State _____ Zip _____

Frontiers of Faith

Kay Cornelius

___Sign of the Bow___—Hours after the first warning of trouble, Sara Craighead, surrounded by Seneca warriors, is on a forced march through the dense woods. Her little brother was kidnapped by another group of Seneca, and Sarah has no idea whether her parents are dead or alive. HP87 $2.95

___Sign of the Eagle___—Young and strong, Adam leaves his wilderness home to discover what work God has called him to. Adam's long blond hair and buckskin clothing cut a dashing figure on Philadelphia's streets and attract attention from two of the most eligible young women in the city. HP91 $2.95

___Sign of the Dove___—As the end of war returns peace to Carolina, Hannah finds herself fighting a new battle in her heart. Not only must she determine her true feelings for Clay and Nate, but she also must resolve the anger and bitterness she harbors toward her cousin Marie. HP95 $2.95

___Sign of the Spirit___—Coming Soon!

···· Hearts ♥ng ····

Any 12 *Heartsong Presents* titles for only $26.95 *

HISTORICAL ROMANCE IS CHEAPER BY THE DOZEN!

Buy any assortment of twelve *Heartsong Presents* titles and save 25% off of the already discounted price of $2.95 each!

*plus $1.00 shipping and handling per order and sales tax where applicable.

HEARTSONG PRESENTS TITLES AVAILABLE NOW:

__HP 7 CANDLESHINE, *Colleen L. Reece*
__HP 8 DESERT ROSE, *Colleen L. Reece*
__HP 12 COTTONWOOD DREAMS, *Norene Morris*
__HP 15 WHISPERS ON THE WIND, *Maryn Langer*
__HP 16 SILENCE IN THE SAGE, *Colleen L. Reece*
__HP 23 GONE WEST, *Kathleen Karr*
__HP 24 WHISPERS IN THE WILDERNESS, *Colleen L. Reece*
__HP 27 BEYOND THE SEARCHING RIVER, *Jacquelyn Cook*
__HP 28 DAKOTA DAWN, *Lauraine Snelling*
__HP 31 DREAM SPINNER, *Sally Laity*
__HP 32 THE PROMISED LAND, *Kathleen Karr*
__HP 35 WHEN COMES THE DAWN, *Brenda Bancroft*
__HP 36 THE SURE PROMISE, *JoAnn A. Grote*
__HP 39 RAINBOW HARVEST, *Norene Morris*
__HP 40 PERFECT LOVE, *Janelle Jamison*
__HP 43 VEILED JOY, *Colleen L. Reece*
__HP 44 DAKOTA DREAM, *Lauraine Snelling*
__HP 47 TENDER JOURNEYS, *Janelle Jamison*
__HP 48 SHORES OF DELIVERANCE, *Kate Blackwell*
__HP 51 THE UNFOLDING HEART, *JoAnn A. Grote*
__HP 52 TAPESTRY OF TAMAR, *Colleen L. Reece*
__HP 55 TREASURE OF THE HEART, *JoAnn A. Grote*
__HP 56 A LIGHT IN THE WINDOW, *Janelle Jamison*
__HP 59 EYES OF THE HEART, *Maryn Langer*
__HP 60 MORE THAN CONQUERORS, *Kay Cornelius*
__HP 63 THE WILLING HEART, *Janelle Jamison*
__HP 64 CROWS'-NESTS AND MIRRORS, *Colleen L. Reece*
__HP 67 DAKOTA DUSK, *Lauraine Snelling*
__HP 68 RIVERS RUSHING TO THE SEA, *Jacquelyn Cook*
__HP 71 DESTINY'S ROAD, *Janelle Jamison*
__HP 72 SONG OF CAPTIVITY, *Linda Herring*
__HP 75 MUSIC IN THE MOUNTAINS, *Colleen L. Reece*
__HP 76 HEARTBREAK TRAIL, *VeraLee Wiggins*

(If ordering from this page, please remember to include it with the order form.)

······ Presents ······

Great Inspirational Romance at a Great Price!

Heartsong Presents books are inspirational romances in contemporary and historical settings, designed to give you an enjoyable, spirit-lifting reading experience. You can choose from 124 wonderfully written titles from some of today's best authors like Colleen L. Reece, Brenda Bancroft, Janelle Jamison, and many others.

When ordering quantities less than twelve, above titles are $2.95 each.

Heartsong Presents
Love Stories Are Rated G!

That's for godly, gratifying, and of course, great! If you love a thrilling love story, but don't appreciate the sordidness of popular paperback romances, **Heartsong Presents** is for you. In fact, **Heartsong Presents** is the *only inspirational romance book club*, the only one featuring love stories where Christian faith is the primary ingredient in a marriage relationship.

Sign up today to receive your first set of four, never before published Christian romances. Send no money now; you will receive a bill with the first shipment. You may cancel at any time without obligation, and if you aren't completely satisfied with any selection, you may return the books for an immediate refund!

Imagine. . .four new romances every month—two historical, two contemporary—with men and women like you who long to meet the one God has chosen as the love of their lives. . .all for the low price of $9.97 postpaid.

To join, simply complete the coupon below and mail to the address provided. **Heartsong Presents** romances are rated G for another reason: They'll arrive *Godspeed!*